WILL TO LIVE

A DETECTIVE KAY HUNTER NOVEL

RACHEL AMPHLETT

SAXON
PUBLISHING

CHAPTER ONE

Elsa Flanagan cursed under her breath and slapped the side of the torch against the palm of her hand.

The beam wavered before it flickered back to life and she exhaled, releasing some of the tension from her shoulders.

She'd told Dennis to change the batteries the previous evening when he'd returned from the pub, the dog carrying a faint scent of cigarette smoke from where his owner had passed the time with his friends in the small undercover shelter to the side of the fourteenth-century tavern.

He'd obviously forgotten all about the batteries after several pints of real ale, and now she was traipsing across the pitch black field with Smokey, praying the beam held out long enough for her to let the dog have a quick trot around before she headed home for the evening.

Early spring, and the air was laden with a freshness,

the countryside beginning to waken from its winter slumber.

She'd spent the afternoon in the garden, pulling out all the old and rotten vegetation, the roses receiving a vicious pruning, and the flowerbeds prepped and ready for the first burst of daffodils.

Dennis had phoned half an hour ago and said he'd be late home from the golf course. There had been a crash on the M20 where the new merging lanes, implemented the previous year, still caused grief for unsuspecting drivers.

Elsa had huffed, but knew it wasn't his fault. They enjoyed their evening walks with the dog together, but he'd urged her to go on without him this time.

'Goodness knows how long I'll be,' he'd said.

Reluctantly, she'd agreed with him, as Smokey was already pacing the hallway in anticipation.

'Come on, then,' she'd said, grabbing his lead from its position on the newel post, and headed out, locking the front door behind her.

There was a time when she'd have simply let the dog wait until the morning for a long walk and let him out into the garden instead, but with his advancing years she knew if she didn't take him now he'd be unsettled all night, and she wouldn't get any sleep.

Dennis would be too busy snoring to notice.

She'd smiled and waved at a neighbour returning from walking her Yorkshire Terrier, and then turned and followed an overgrown footpath that led to a small field.

As far as she was aware, only the neighbour used

the route regularly. She and Dennis normally walked along a different path that took them past the village pub. Their suburb was far enough out of the main town to be uncrowded, and for the most part was populated by people who were retired, or whose children had left the nest long ago. She'd let the dog off his lead the moment she reached the barren field, safe in the knowledge the area was well-fenced. She trusted him to come back when called, but it was reassuring to know he couldn't stray onto the railway line that cut through the end of the field while he was chasing rabbits.

Conscious of the darkening sky, she'd rummaged in her pocket and pulled out the small torch, and it was then she realised Dennis had forgotten to change the batteries.

Now, she wished she had taken the time to check before leaving the house.

An excited bark from Smokey jerked her back to the present. His silhouette bounded across the field beyond where she stood with the lead in her hand, a flash of white near the hedgerow beyond reflecting off the torch's beam as a rabbit made a lucky escape.

In the distance, and still several miles away, the sound of the horn of the 5.55 from London Victoria carried on the wind. There was a time, not so long ago, when the sound acted as an alarm clock for her, a signal to switch on the oven and start preparing dinner ready for when Dennis walked through the front door, having driven from the railway station.

Now, she emitted a two-note whistle to the dog and jangled the metal clasp of his lead.

The rabbit out of reach, the dog scampered back towards her.

Tutting under her breath at the sight of his mud-covered paws, she clipped the lead to his collar and ruffled the fur between his ears.

'Good boy.'

He strained at the lead as she straightened, his head swivelling towards the railway line, and pricked his ears.

A breeze tugged at her hair, and she frowned.

'Come on, all the rabbits are gone.'

She turned to go but the lead grew taut.

Glancing down, she saw the Border Collie staring at the tracks, his body rigid. His ears twitched, and he lifted his nose into the air before he whined and strained at the lead once more.

'What is it?'

She felt a pang of fear. Dennis was always telling her not to walk the dog over the field by herself. "You're too trusting", he said. "It's not like the old days", he said. "Take him around the block instead".

She waved the torch in a wide circle, the faint beam falling on a pair of rabbits that turned and fled as the light fell upon them.

'It's only rabbits, Smokey,' she scolded, while trying to ignore the tremor in her voice. 'Come—'

The wind brushed her cheek, and she heard it then.

A faint voice, male.

Smokey whined again before he growled, a rumble that started in his throat and ended in a low bark.

'Who's there?'

She heard the tremble in her voice, and patted the pockets of her jacket, her heart racing.

Dammit.

She'd left her mobile phone on the kitchen counter in her haste to walk the dog before it grew too dark to navigate the field.

She took a step back and tugged on the lead.

'Smokey. Come on.'

He whined again, and instead of following her, pulled forward.

She stumbled, managed to regain her balance at the last moment, and inhaled sharply.

'Help me.'

Elsa craned her neck, trying to see beyond the farthest reaches of the torch beam.

The voice appeared to be coming from the direction of the railway line.

She took a few steps forward and, emboldened, the dog took up the slack and pulled once more.

'Hello?'

A moment's pause, then—

'Help! Please – somebody help me!'

Her heart hammering, Elsa began to hurry across the uneven ground, and cried out as her ankle turned. She kept her balance, ignored the painful twinge from her arthritic hip, and made her way down the gentle slope towards the tracks.

A tangle of vines covered a wire mesh fence that had been erected between the field and the railway, and she paced beside it until she found an area that was less densely covered in vegetation.

She couldn't climb the fence, not with her hip, and with her short stature, the top of it reached a half head above her.

'Please, help me – I can't move!'

She waved her torch in the direction of the voice, her breath escaping her lips in short bursts, until the beam fell upon a length of material that lay across the tracks.

She blinked, and then the material moved.

'The train's coming! Help me!'

Elsa cried out, and covered her mouth with her hand, before dropping the torch. Close up, she could still make out the wriggling form.

A rumble in the ground sent a small shockwave up her legs, and her head jerked to the right.

Smokey began to bark, excited by the roar of the approaching train, and the man's terrified screams.

'Oh God, oh God.'

Elsa wrapped her fingers around the mesh of the metal fencing and tried to prise it from the post, but it wouldn't yield. Her breath escaped in short, panicked gasps as she rattled the wire mesh in an attempt to find a weak point, a way through.

The man continued to squirm, his body against the nearest rail, and his head furthest away from her.

'Get up, get up!' she urged. 'The train's coming!'

Why isn't he moving?

Only metres away from where she stood, the rails began their familiar song as the weight of the train's wheels bore down, coming closer.

The horn sounded once more.

The man began to scream, begging her to hurry, to stop the train, to help him, but the wire refused to yield under her touch.

The train rounded the corner, its light bearing down on her, and she lifted her gaze to the rails.

The man had managed to raise his head, and was staring at her, terrified.

The train's brakes squealed as the headlights picked out the form in its path, but it wasn't going to stop in time. It was simply too heavy and going too fast.

Elsa screwed up her eyes in a vain attempt to shut out the vision before her, a moment too late.

The man's screams were drowned out by a sickening crunch, blood exploding across the front of the locomotive.

The wheels screeched against the rails as the train shuddered to a halt, the ensuing silence only broken by the hiss of air brakes.

The dog whined once before pushing its trembling body against her legs, and then Elsa turned and vomited into the undergrowth.

CHAPTER TWO

Detective Sergeant Kay Hunter pulled the car in behind a white four-wheel drive vehicle emblazoned with the British Transport Police logos across its paintwork, and swallowed.

A death on a railway was never easy to deal with, and she'd only had to attend a scene such as this once before in her career – a long time ago, when she was still a police constable.

It was something she'd hoped she wouldn't have to repeat.

The phone call had come in as the team were starting to leave for the day, with a request from those at the scene to have two detectives attend. Details were scant, but the transport police had been at the scene for the past forty minutes, and the railway owners were keen to reopen the line as soon as possible.

'Rush hour. Inconsiderate bastard,' one of the older detectives had muttered. 'Glad it's you, not me.'

Now, Kay turned to the woman in the passenger seat next to her.

Detective Constable Carys Miles stared wide-eyed through the windscreen, her usually pale face a deathly shade of white.

'Think yourself lucky – you're not the one who has to clear this up.'

'That doesn't help.'

'Come on. Let's go.'

A motley collection of ambulances, buses and police vehicles were parked either side of the narrow country road. A uniformed officer stood at an open gate set within a hedgerow, directing attending services towards an unpaved track that led away from the lane and across a field. Floodlights created a pool of light the length of it, and as Kay followed the path with her eyes, she saw the train and its eight carriages of trapped commuters on the railway beyond.

'Evening, Graham,' said Kay, as she approached.

'Hello, Sarge.'

'Who's in charge of the scene?'

The constable pointed across to the small crowd gathered at the bottom of the field. 'Dave Walker, British Transport Police. He's the one who requested we attend.'

'Okay. Let's go see what he's got.'

Kay led the way along the track, careful to avoid the muddier parts of the field.

'This bloody railway,' she muttered under her

breath. 'The fencing was supposed to stop this sort of thing happening.'

'Is it common here?' asked Carys, as she hurried to keep up.

'Put it this way, the locals called it the "Suicide Mile" for years. It calmed down for a bit once the fencing went up eighteen months ago, but I guess if someone's determined to end their life—'

'There has to be a better way to go.'

'You'd think so, right?'

A man broke away from the group of police officers as they approached, his face shadowed by the angle of the floodlights.

'Detective Sergeant Kay Hunter?'

'That's me.'

He held out his hand. 'Sergeant Dave Walker.'

Kay introduced Carys, and then gestured towards the track. 'Another suicide?'

'We're not sure, and that's why you're here. According to an eyewitness, the victim tried to change his mind at the last minute.'

'What do you mean?'

'She's with one of your constables at the moment, giving a statement.' He jabbed his thumb over his shoulder. 'Pretty shaken up, as you can imagine. Apparently, she was out walking her dog when she heard a man's voice. She wandered down here to investigate, and said he was calling out to her for help. She couldn't get over the fence to reach him in time.'

Kay glanced over her shoulder as one of the attending ambulances started to drive away across the field, bumping and jerking over the uneven ground towards a gate that had been opened on the far side.

'They didn't hang around to declare life extinct?'

'No need.' He pointed to a small, white tent that had been erected the other side of the fence amongst the undergrowth some metres away from the front of the train. 'His head's over there.'

Carys emitted a groan and turned away.

'Current status?'

'We're waiting for confirmation from the control centre that the line's safe and no locomotives are shunting between stations, and then we'll start to get these people off the train and onto the buses. All other passenger trains have been stopped at stations either side of our location, so there are buses running between Maidstone and Tonbridge. It's a mess.'

'How long do you think it'll be before you get your confirmation we're good to go?'

'Should be within the next fifteen minutes.'

'Okay, thanks. We'll go have a chat with the witness ourselves in the meantime.'

Kay walked side by side with Carys as they approached one of the patrol vehicles, the back door open. Inside, the figure of a diminutive, older woman sat huddled on the back seat, her eyes wide as she spoke to the police officer standing beside the vehicle, notebook in hand.

A Border Collie sat at her feet, his ears attentive as she spoke, but sensed the two detectives approaching and twisted round to meet them, straining at his lead.

Kay bent down to pat the dog on the head, then straightened and waited while the uniformed officer introduced them to Elsa Flanagan.

'I've finished taking Mrs Flanagan's initial statement,' she said. 'I'll have it on your desk by the morning. Mrs Flanagan's husband is on his way to collect her. He should be here soon.'

'Thank you,' said Kay, as she turned her attention to the older woman and crouched down. 'Mrs Flanagan, I realise that you've spent time with my colleague here going over the events of this evening, but would you mind telling me what happened?'

The woman exhaled, a shaking breath that spoke volumes, and pulled the blanket tighter around her shoulders.

'It was terrible,' she said. 'I had no idea there was someone down here. I was walking Smokey, and he was busy chasing rabbits, and then when I called him, he came running. It wasn't until I'd put his lead on that he heard something. I thought he was being difficult, but then I heard a voice. Down here.'

'Where were you when you first heard the voice?'

'There. About halfway up the field, where that dip in the landscape is. See it?'

Kay shielded her eyes from the bright floodlights, and picked out the area the woman indicated on the fringes of the taped-off area. 'Yes.'

'There's a footpath just beyond. Leads back to the road where we live. There's only us and another woman who use it to walk our dogs.'

'You didn't see anyone else when you set out?'

'Only the woman who was out walking before me. She's got a Yorkshire Terrier.'

Kay glanced at the police officer, who nodded. 'We've got a note of the neighbour's details,' she said. 'PC West left twenty minutes ago to go and speak to her.'

'Thanks.' Kay turned her attention back to Elsa. 'What happened, after you first heard the man's voice?'

'I thought it was a mugger or someone. Dennis is always telling me not to come down here on my own. Prefers me to walk Smokey around the block if he's not back to walk with me.' She leaned forward and ruffled the dog's ears. 'But Smokey likes it down here.'

Kay waited. The witness was processing her memories of the accident, and she had no wish to rush her. The poor woman was traumatised enough as it was.

Elsa sighed and sat back on the passenger seat, her eyes downcast. 'Smokey wouldn't budge. Kept pulling on the lead, as if he knew something was wrong. Then I heard it. He called out. "Help me", he said. At first, I didn't know where the voice was coming from, but then he called out again and I realised the voice was coming from down here, near the railway line.' She brought a shaking hand to her mouth. 'I heard the train horn, then. You can hear it as it leaves East Malling station if the wind's in the right direction. I ran, well as fast as I could, to the bottom of the field, where the fence is. I couldn't see anything at first, and kept shining the torch around, but then he moved.'

'Where was he, exactly?'

'Across the tracks, at an angle. His feet were nearest to me, and his head was on the other side.'

'Okay. Go on.'

'I couldn't get over the fence. I have arthritis in my hip, and the fence was too high. I tried to pull the mesh, to loosen it, but I couldn't. The train was getting closer, and all the time, he's crying out for help. Then the train came round the corner. I don't know – I suppose by then the driver could see him because the headlight nearly blinded me, but he couldn't stop. He didn't stop—'

Kay placed her hand on the woman's knee. 'Thank you, Elsa.'

'Sarge? Looks like Mr Flanagan is here.'

Kay straightened at Carys's voice, and came face to face with a man in his seventies, his face ashen.

'Elsa?'

The woman thrust the blanket aside as the dog spun round and launched himself at the man. The woman fell into the man's arms, and his eyes met Kay's.

'Can I take her home now?'

'Yes.' Kay handed one of her business cards to the couple. 'Thank you, Mrs Flanagan. We'll be in touch over the next day or so, but please – if you need to talk to someone, please seek help. You've witnessed a very traumatic event, and these things take time.'

'Thank you, Detective.'

Kay watched as the older couple moved towards the floodlit track and then turned as Sergeant Walker approached.

'We've got the all clear,' he said. 'I'll show you what we've got.'

Kay and Carys followed him as he led the way towards a gap that had been severed in the fence line to allow the emergency services and investigating teams to access the railway tracks.

A steady stream of disgruntled passengers was being discharged from the carriage at the far end, away from the carnage at the front of the train.

'Where's the driver?' she asked as she pulled on the coveralls and plastic booties that were handed to her.

'Giving his statement to one of my colleagues,' he said. 'We'll have a copy of that over to you as soon as possible.'

'Ta.'

'Jesus.'

Kay acknowledged Carys's murmured comment as they approached the front of the train.

Blood spatter covered the front wheels, a tangled mess of clothing and limbs strewn underneath.

Kay checked over her shoulder.

The first responders had erected shields at the start of the carriages, so none of the passengers would be able to see what was going on at the business end of the investigation.

'Harriet's here,' said Carys.

Kay greeted the head of the Crime Scene

Investigation team and explained the known facts while the woman pulled a set of protective coveralls over her own clothes and tied her hair back.

An astute and respected CSI, Harriet Baker had studied at Oxford before taking up residence in the Kent county town with her sales manager husband and had worked with Kay on a number of cases.

Her face grim, she gestured to the photographer that joined her.

'If we're all ready, let's take a quick look, and then I'm locking down this crime scene for processing. I'd prefer it if only one of you accompanied us,' she said to Kay.

Kay took one look at Carys's pale face and wide eyes and knew she'd have to go.

'Makes sense. Carys – if you could wait here, and then liaise with Harriet's team for the rest of this evening?'

'Yes, Sarge,' said the detective constable, the relief in her voice palpable before she scurried away.

'Someone changing their mind about committing suicide isn't unusual,' said Kay. 'So, what do you need us for?'

Walker beckoned to her and the CSI and then made his way to the rear of the locomotive via a demarcated path that had been erected above the troughing route caused by the ballast, the photographer trailing in their wake. He crouched beside the wheels and shone his torch onto the tracks. 'It wasn't suicide.'

Kay gulped at the mess, but tried to focus on the task at hand. 'What am I looking for?'

In reply, Walker wiggled the torch beam across the far rail.

'There. What's left of his ankles is tied to the tracks.'

CHAPTER THREE

Kay elbowed the door to the incident room open, balancing a pile of manilla folders she'd brought from her usual work desk, and trying not to let the strap of her handbag slip down her arm.

'Here. I've got it.'

She glanced up at the familiar voice. 'Hi, Gavin – thanks.'

She stuck her foot against the door so the young police officer could follow, his arms laden with stationery supplies and an assortment of textbooks, and then made her way over to a desk on one side of the room.

Screens and computer hard drives had already been laid out at each desk by the IT team, and as PC Gavin Piper moved around the room plugging in keyboards and switching each of the machines on, the rest of the immediate team began to arrive.

The door swung open and Ian Barnes appeared, a

detective constable that Kay had known for years. After a brief sabbatical, he'd phoned Kay a few weeks ago to say he'd be returning to the station, and she looked forward to working with him once more. He could be abrupt, but Kay enjoyed his dry sense of humour.

He grinned as he approached her desk. 'Long time, no see, Hunter.'

'Good to have you back, Ian.'

'Ah, you say that now.'

She shook her head and smiled. 'I bagged you this one,' she said, pointing to the desk abutting hers. 'That okay?'

'Yeah – I can steal your stuff more easily.'

'Great.'

He threw his jacket over the back of his chair and stretched. 'Where's Sharp?'

'In with Larch and the chief super. Should be here any minute.'

Kay took the steaming takeout cup of coffee he held out to her, and leaned back in her chair. 'Thanks.'

'Figured you'd need it. What time did you get home last night?'

'About eleven.'

'Adam around?'

'Already asleep. He was still snoring his head off when I left this morning.'

'Lucky bastard,' said the older detective. 'If I'd known I was going to be called in today, I wouldn't have offered to pick Emma up from that bloody boy band gig in London at one o'clock in the morning.'

Kay grinned and pulled out a chair from under the desk next to him. 'You love it really.'

He smiled and popped open the top of the Styrofoam cup. 'Yeah,' he conceded, and stifled a yawn before taking a sip.

'Could be worse, Ian – she could've asked you to go to the concert with her.'

He choked and punched his fist against his chest before speaking. 'That's not funny.'

Kay laughed, reached across the desk and wiggled the mouse to bring the two computer monitors to life. 'Have you seen Carys?'

'Yes, she was in before you. On to her third coffee, I think.'

'I've asked her to liaise with Harriet on this one. Thought it'd do her good.'

'Good call. Much left?'

Kay wrinkled her nose and put down her coffee. 'I don't envy Lucas and his colleagues at the best of times, let alone with one like this. As for the ambulance and fire service lads that had to clean up afterwards—'

'I heard he was decapitated.'

'Yeah.'

'At least it was quick.'

'Apart from the fact he knew it was going to happen.'

Kay turned her attention back to the files, sorting them into the trays next to her computer. No matter if she now had a murder case to solve, she would still have to try to stay on top of the myriad of crimes that needed to be followed up and processed. Nobody else was available.

She didn't look up when Detective Inspector Sharp entered the room, his pace business-like as he strode towards the whiteboard that Piper had set up ready for the investigation to begin.

Instead, she finished arranging her desk the way she wanted it as a way to ready herself for the adrenalin and frustration that she knew the investigation would bring.

'Right, gather round,' said Sharp.

Kay turned her seat to face the whiteboard, then swallowed.

Detective Chief Inspector Angus Larch stood next to Sharp, his eyes boring into hers.

CHAPTER FOUR

Kay had managed to avoid Larch since the last murder investigation when they'd crossed paths. Upon solving the case and ensuring two nasty individuals were put behind bars for producing and distributing snuff films, Larch had grudgingly congratulated her for her efforts but since then, he'd continued to block and delay any attempt of hers to be promoted to detective inspector, citing a Professional Standards investigation she'd been subjected to the previous year.

Common sense had won through in the end though, and the investigation had confirmed her innocence, something that she'd maintained all along.

It had wreaked havoc on her health, though and she kept the secret of a subsequent miscarriage from her colleagues. Instead she and her other half, Adam, had kept to themselves, battled through, and carried on.

Yet Larch continued to question her professional abilities at every opportunity.

It appeared as though his role had taken a toll on him recently, however. Bags protruded under bloodshot eyes, and the broken veins that cast a spidery pattern over the bridge of his nose appeared more pronounced. Despite this, she had little sympathy for him.

Two men stood by the whiteboard next to them, and Kay recognised one from the previous night. The other, she didn't know.

She dropped her gaze, twisted round to pick up her notebook, and concentrated on taking notes as Sharp began the briefing.

'Let's make a start.' He waited while the assembled team drew closer. 'Before we begin, I'd like to introduce Sergeants Dave Walker and Robert Moss from British Transport Police. Given the nature of this death, and their combined knowledge of the location, we'll be sharing resources on this one. Introduce yourselves after the briefing, make them welcome.'

His comments were met with a chorus of mumbles of agreement while the two BTP officers found seats and faced the whiteboard.

'Right, Hunter – bring us up to speed with the events of last night.'

Kay stood and wandered over to the front of the room, and provided an overview of the known facts before concluding. 'We're treating this death as suspicious, as our eyewitness says the victim called out for help, and he was unable to move from the railway line before the train hit him. When attending the scene,

Sergeant Walker and his colleagues noticed that the victim's ankles had been tied to the tracks.'

A shocked silence filled the room.

'DCI Larch and I met with the Chief Superintendent prior to this meeting to discuss the media strategy,' said Sharp. 'At the present time, we'll be reporting it to the public as a possible suicide, and inform them that police enquiries are continuing. Until further notice, we won't be alerting them to the fact we are investigating a murder. We don't want to let the perpetrator or anyone else involved know we're on to them.'

'You've got to admit, it's the perfect disguise for a killer,' said Kay. 'Any victim of this type of murder would be considered another suicide statistic.'

'We're not saying all of the suicides on that stretch of track are murder victims, Hunter,' said Larch.

Kay bit her lip. The man's voice appeared raspy as if he was coming down with a cold or had been talking too much. She took a deep breath. 'I realise that, sir, but I do think it's worth bearing in mind.'

'I think it's a good idea.'

Kay twisted around in her chair to see Carys staring at Larch, her chin jutting out, then turned back.

'This was too well thought out,' she said. 'It gives me the impression whoever the killer is, he's done it before.'

'I'm inclined to agree with Hunter,' said Sharp. 'The last thing we want to contemplate is a killer having gone unnoticed for so long, but we can't rule it out. Not at this stage.'

Larch glowered at Kay, but she refused to look away. Finally, he sighed. 'Well, it's your reputation on the line, Sharp. I'll let you get on with it.'

He stalked from the room.

Sharp waited until the door slammed shut behind the detective chief inspector, then gestured to Carys. 'Initial findings from Harriet?'

The detective constable opened her notebook and cleared her throat. 'The victim was decapitated. The force of the train hitting him severed his head, which was found in the undergrowth next to the locomotive.'

A collective groan filled the room, and Kay noted a few mutters of thanks from those who were spared from having to attend the scene.

'There's not much left of the victim's body. We have the remains of the legs – the parts Sergeant Walker's team found tied to the track. His other limbs are badly damaged.'

Sharp nodded. 'To be expected. Hunter – when does Lucas think he'll be able to let us have his initial findings?'

'This morning,' said Kay. 'He knows we're counting on him to help us identify the victim, so he's trying to accelerate the post mortem. Lucky for us, it's been a quiet couple of days elsewhere.'

'What about the surrounding area – vehicles, reported sightings of suspicious activity?' Sharp aimed his question at the BTP officers.

'None yet,' said Walker. 'Your CSI team cordoned off the area opposite where Mrs Flanagan says she was standing. They've found partial footprints in the dirt below the level of the railway tracks, and the undergrowth has been trampled, so they'll take samples from there as well.'

'We've drawn up a schedule of nearby residents and pubs, that sort of thing. We'll work with uniform to gather as many statements as possible over the next few days,' said Kay.

Sharp checked his watch. 'Okay, well as we're in limbo until Harriet gives us something to work with, let's get on with what we've got. We'll get admin to work with BTP and pull out the records of all other suicides along that stretch. Given the nature of this one, we're going to have to check whether this is a one-off or not. Barnes, head over to the Flanagans' house and speak with Elsa. See if she can recall anything new from last night. After that, go and speak to the other dog walker – the one with the Yorkshire Terrier. It was lighter when she was walking her dog, she might have seen someone near the tracks.'

'Guv.'

'Carys, head over to Harriet's lab. Find out if they've got anything from the victim's clothing, anything at all that might give us a head start or help us identify him before her report comes in. Kay, you're on the post mortem – if Lucas says he's going to do it this morning given the circumstances, let's not keep him waiting. Debbie – liaise with uniform and go through the other statements from last night from local residents and coordinate the schedule Kay mentioned. Identify the gaps, see if anyone noticed anything unusual, and find out who we need to talk to again. Establish a pattern for enquiries and liaise with me early afternoon to update me.'

'Yes, guv.' The young police officer lowered her head and wrote in her notebook, her brow furrowed in concentration.

Kay smiled. Debbie West was another rising star, and an asset to the investigation.

Sharp checked his watch. 'Afternoon debrief at four o'clock, people. Don't be late.'

Kay waited until the team dispersed, then made her way over to where Carys sat.

'Hey.'

'Hi, Kay.'

She pulled out a spare chair and scooted it closer to the detective constable's before lowering her voice.

'Listen, I know you want to make a good impression, but trust me – taking on Larch in my defence isn't a good idea.'

The other woman's smile wavered. 'What do you mean?'

'I appreciate the gesture but, please – don't do it again.'

She managed a smile of her own to soften her words, and moved away.

It was better for everyone if she fought her own battles.

CHAPTER FIVE

'Sarge?'

She aimed the key fob at the car and then caught up with Gavin. 'What?'

'I've never been to a post mortem.'

Kay led the way across the car park to a side door to the building. She held the door open, then put up her hand to stop him. 'Shallow breaths. Think about the investigation, not what you're about to see.'

He swallowed. 'Sarge.'

She headed towards a reception desk and signed them both in. Taking the coveralls that were handed to her, she handed one set to Gavin and walked towards a set of double doors.

'You can use the male locker room to pop these on,' she said. 'Leave all your personal belongings in one of the lockers, there should be plenty free.' Kay pointed over his shoulder. 'Toilets are there, if you need them.'

'Thanks. I think.'

Moments later, he joined her at the double doors, and she gave a thin smile.

'Let's get this over with.'

'Morning, Hunter,' said Lucas, as they entered the room. 'Sharp said you'd be on your way.'

'And he said to convey his thanks for getting this one done so quickly.'

'Well, there's not much left of him, so it made sense to get him out of the way first. We've made a start, as we needed some specialist help that was only available first thing this morning.'

Kay introduced Gavin and moved around the examination table. 'Found much?'

Lucas gestured to the limbs that had been set out on the table. 'Not much from these, unfortunately. No tattoos, no scars – and no sign of surgery, so we can rule out finding anything like steel plates to trace him.' He moved the mangled hand to one side.

'You'll email photos of his face to us, so we can get a couple of admins to start going through the missing persons database?'

'I'll arrange to have them sent over as soon as we're finished here.'

'It's not much to go on, is it? Feels like this case is going to be a long slog.'

'Not necessarily. We had a bit more luck with the skull, look,' said Lucas. He rolled the severed head over so the mouth faced them.

Kay concentrated on what he was showing her, refusing to look at the victim's eyes.

Lucas used his thumbs to prise open the mouth, while his assistant tilted the overhead light to shine into the cavity. 'When a person is decapitated, the loss of blood is so sudden, rigor mortis doesn't set in. We wouldn't be able to do this for a few days otherwise. Here, you can see he's had some significant dental work done over the years. His back molars are extremely worn down, as if he's grinding his teeth. Evidence of stress, that sort of thing. But it's recent wear and tear. Also, he's had two teeth removed at some point. You see these two here? They're false, pinned in under surgery.'

'So you'll be able to identify him?'

'Eventually. The forensic odontologist has been – you just missed her. She's taken X-rays and made some plaster of Paris impressions of the jaw as well as a physical count of teeth placement. We'll speak to Missing Persons and local dentists. No two people have the same odontology profile, so hopefully we'll hear something within the week. At the moment, all I can tell you is that he was aged between thirty-five and fifty years old.'

'Anything else?'

'As you can imagine, there wasn't much left of his torso. It took the full brunt of the impact. We've taken swabs from under what's left of his fingernails. His left hand was no good to us at all, but we have three fingers of his right hand to work with. There's a slight indentation on the middle finger, perhaps from a signet ring or something, but unless Harriet's team find the ring, that's about it. We've taken fingerprints where we can, but unfortunately there's not enough left for a full set.'

'We'll run what you've got through the database, see if we can figure out who he is that way. If he hasn't been in trouble before though, it won't help us.'

Kay resisted the temptation to inhale. She had learnt from experience that the taste from a shocked intake of breath would haunt her for the rest of the afternoon, the stench within the morgue was so acute. Instead, she gestured to the mangled remains set out on the examination table. "What else can you tell us about him?"

Lucas's lips thinned. 'Not much, I'm afraid,' he said. 'Unless, or until, we get some results back on those jaw X-rays and impressions, or you receive a call from a relative wondering where he is, he's going to remain a mystery. We'll continue here for another hour or so, but I don't think we'll find anything else.'

'Thanks, Lucas.'

Kay led the way out of the room and headed for the door to the ladies' locker room. 'I'll meet you out here once you've had a chance to get changed,' she said, over her shoulder to Gavin.

She pulled her bag from the secure cabinet, removed the paper coveralls provided by the morgue team, and shoved them into the biohazard bin next to the door before wrenching it open.

Gavin paced the corridor outside, his face pale.

'Okay, let's go.'

Gavin burst through the door, held it open for Kay,

and then shoved his hands in his pockets and tipped his head to the sky, closed his eyes and took a deep breath.

'Okay?'

'Yeah. Give me a minute.'

'Don't be embarrassed. I nearly puked the first time, and that was even though I saw dead bodies while I was still in uniform.'

He opened his eyes. 'I still might.'

She grinned, reached into her bag, and pulled out a packet of mints. 'Here. Have one of these.'

He took them from her, ripped out a mint, and handed it back. 'Do they help?'

'No, but it'll give you something to do while I drive.'

He followed her to the car. 'It's okay for you. You didn't bat an eyelid in there.'

Kay shrugged as she unlocked it and climbed in. 'It doesn't mean it doesn't affect me. But over time, you learn to focus on what you're finding out while you're there, and how it can help you solve the case. That helps to get you through the experience, because you never know when you might be listening to someone over the next few days, or reading something about the victim's background that will link to something you've seen or heard during the post mortem. A pathologist's report can only tell you so much. That's why it's important we attend. We get the chance to ask Lucas questions straight away, and between us we might find something that would otherwise have been overlooked. It's a team effort.'

'Does it get any better?'

'Easier, you mean? No. Not really. But you'll find your own way of working through it.'

He swallowed the last of the mint and his eyes hardened. 'What sort of bastard would do that to someone?'

Kay turned the key in the ignition. 'Let's find out.'

CHAPTER SIX

By the time Kay returned to the incident room, the team had received a series of computerised files containing all recorded instances of suicides on railway tracks in the area.

'We'll start with the last five years,' said Sharp, pacing his office as he waited for the files to be uploaded onto the database for the investigation. 'We still have no identification for our victim, but at least Lucas has got a rough estimate of age for us. It's not much to start with, but separate out the records and put anyone who matches those criteria to one side. Those are the ones we'll concentrate on to start with.'

Kay twisted in her seat as he stalked behind her once more. 'Guv? Could you sit down? I'm getting a crick in my neck trying to keep up with you.'

He sighed and sank into his chair. 'Better?'

'Yes, thanks. I was going to suggest that once we have those particular cases split up, we divide them into identified victims and ones like ours – the unknowns. Then try to establish if anyone on the missing persons database is a match.'

'Get Debbie and one of the admin team members on to that as soon as possible. Once they've identified the ones that have names then you, Barnes, and Carys can start contacting the families.'

'I'd like to get Gavin involved, too, guv.'

'His detective exams are coming up, so make sure he doesn't get too distracted.' His gaze drifted through the partition windows to the incident room where the young police officer sat. 'I have a feeling he's got a promising career ahead of him. He certainly doesn't mind putting in the effort.'

'I think there's a bit of rivalry going on between him and Carys.' Kay smiled. 'That should make things interesting.'

'True. Make sure it doesn't get in the way of this investigation, though.'

'Will do.'

'All right. Let's get the briefing underway.'

He led the way out to the incident room, and Kay plucked a spare seat out from under a desk.

'Right,' said Sharp. 'Barnes – give us an update on your trip over to see Harriet.'

Barnes gestured to Carys, who cleared her throat before speaking.

'Harriet confirms the victim's clothing contained no personal effects. No wallet, no watch – and no suicide note. The first responders had marked out a clear path, and no one was permitted to leave the train until the line was secure. The passengers were kept on the train for an additional twenty minutes so screens could be erected and the crime scene established at the front of the train. We can be sure that most of this was undisturbed prior to CSI arriving.'

'Any signs of vehicle tracks or footprints?'

'The undergrowth to the Chapel Street side of the track was processed first,' said Barnes. 'Had to be, so access could be made to where our victim ended up. The first responders undertook a preliminary search when they arrived, and then taped off the path so Harriet and her team could process the rest of it when they got there. After the line had been declared safe, CSI began to process the far side of the track.'

'What did Lucas have to say, Hunter?'

'He's sent X-rays of the man's teeth off for analysis – apparently, the victim had had a major extraction some years ago, and a pair of false teeth were implanted in his gums.'

'Good. With any luck, they'll be able to trace him through those. Time frame?'

'He said a week, but he'll put the pressure on them for a quick result, given the circumstances of death.'

Sharp glanced up at a soft *ping* from one of the computers and Carys moved across the room to read the screen.

'We're ready to go. All the files have been uploaded.'

Kay pushed herself off her chair. 'Let's see what we've got, then.'

They spent the remainder of the afternoon poring over all the information they had received from British Transport Police. The records were thorough, and made for uncomfortable reading.

More than once, Kay had to leave her desk and go for a walk outside simply to clear her head. She hadn't realised there were so many suicide cases each year, let alone the sheer numbers on railways.

A growing sense of frustration about the state of the mental health service and support available to people suffering from depression plagued her thoughts. At one point, Barnes had bumped into her as she opened the side door into the building to return to the incident room.

They shared a knowing look.

'Not the sort of reading material I usually associate with a bright, spring day,' said Barnes. 'Glad to see I'm not the only one who needs to get away from their desk.'

As the sun began to dip below the roof line of the building and cast shadows across her desk, Kay and the rest of the team had established that eight deaths on railway lines around Maidstone bore similar circumstances to that of their investigation.

Barnes and Carys had brought another whiteboard into the incident room, divided it into eight squares, and written up the similarities between the eight suicides and the murder victim.

All were male, and aged between thirty-seven and fifty-two and lived within a fifty-mile radius of the town. Apart from that, the demographics were broad – one man had taken early retirement and could afford to drive a top of the range four-wheel drive, three were unemployed – one returning to live with his mother.

Sharp stood with his hands on his hips staring at the board.

'Good work, everyone. This is a start.' He checked his watch. 'Split these up into two lots. Kay, take Barnes with you in the morning and make arrangements to speak to the families of these men and get up-to-date statements. Carys, Gavin – spend the rest of this afternoon familiarising yourselves with the pathology and inquest reports for these deaths so we're ready to hit the ground running when those statements come back. Let's get some traction on this while our killer still believes he's got away with it.'

CHAPTER SEVEN

Kay turned her key in the door and stepped into the warmth of the hallway, the sound of Adam's voice carrying from the kitchen.

She smiled to herself, locked the door and dropped her handbag on the stairs, hung her coat on the newel post and wandered through to find him. As she entered the kitchen, she heard claws scrambling against the tiled floor and gasped as the biggest dog she'd ever seen ambled towards her.

'Hi,' said Adam. 'This is Holly.'

'Hello, Holly,' said Kay and scratched the dog's ears. The Great Dane's head reached her abdomen and the giant beast leaned into her, sending her stockinged feet sliding across the floor. 'Woah, girl. You're heavy. *Really* heavy,' she added as she saw the tell-tale bulge. Her eyes met Adam's. 'When's she due?'

'Next couple of days,' he said. 'I had some time off

in lieu so we figured it'd be best if I brought her home. Quieter,' he added.

'That makes sense.' Kay patted the pregnant pooch's head. 'All right, girl. Let me through. I need a glass of wine.'

Adam finished arranging the dog's bed in a corner of the kitchen, and then pulled a bottle of white burgundy from the refrigerator and filled two glasses before passing one to her.

'Cheers.'

'Cheers,' she said. 'Here's to not coming home to a snake on the loose this time.'

They clinked their glasses together and he grinned.

'He was fine. He didn't do any harm.'

Kay glared at him over her glass until she couldn't hold her laughter any more.

Holly wandered over and leaned against her once more.

'How was your day?' said Adam, lowering himself onto one of the stools next to the central worktop. 'Have you charged anyone yet?'

Kay shook her head. 'Not yet, and I think it'll be a while before we do. We had to spend the day going through all the previous suicide records.' She gently pushed Holly out of the way and sat opposite to Adam, setting down her wineglass on the worktop between them. 'Regardless of this case, I can't believe anyone would be so desperate as to throw themselves under a train.'

'It takes all sorts.'

'True.' She took a sip of her wine. 'How's things at the clinic this week?'

'Apart from this one? Not too bad. The racing stables are quiet for the next couple of weeks. It's all small stuff at the moment. Mostly guinea pigs and hamsters traumatised by the experience of being taken home by kids for the school holidays.' He winked over his wine glass. 'I think most of them are going to need counselling.'

'I think I would, too.'

Holly moved around to Adam's side of the bench and plonked her massive head in his lap. He stroked her ears, and took another sip of his wine.

'How's the other investigation going?'

Kay bit her lip. She'd spent several weeks – months, in fact – going over the facts as she recalled them about a case from the previous year that had backfired upon the whole force, and had nearly led to her dismissal through a Professional Standards investigation.

Her hunger for justice hadn't waned since she was cleared of any wrongdoing, nor had her determination to find out who had set her up, removing vital evidence from a locked room and blaming her, and sending her career and health into free fall.

She and Adam were still coming to terms with the aftermath, and in an attempt to coax her out of her depression, Adam had suggested that she begin her own investigation – covertly, and at home.

She ran her fingers down the stem of her glass and

swirled the base of it in the condensation on the kitchen worktop. 'I've hit a dead end.'

'In what way?'

She leaned back on the stool and sighed. 'I'm waiting until the office is quiet one night so I can access the database without being disturbed. I don't really want to explain to anyone what I'm doing.'

Adam raised an eyebrow. 'Is that wise? Can't they see if you've accessed it?'

'Yes,' she said. 'But I'm thinking it'd be worth the risk. It's only human, to want to know what really happened, isn't it?'

He held her gaze, his expression troubled. 'Could you get into trouble?'

'Any more than I was?' She snorted. 'No. They've cleared me of any wrongdoing.'

'Is it safe?'

She rubbed at her right eye, then took another sip of her wine. 'I think so.'

Adam reached across the worktop, wrapped his hand around hers, and rubbed his thumb across her knuckles. 'Promise me you'll be careful,' he said.

She smiled.

'Promise. Say it.'

'I promise.'

'Thank you.' He squeezed her hand. 'I couldn't bear it if something happened to you.'

Kay's mobile phone began to vibrate on top of the worktop and she checked the number.

'Shit.'

'What's up?'

'It's my mother.'

'I'll get more wine.'

Kay poked her tongue out at him, and held the phone to her ear. 'Hi, Mum.'

'I thought you were never going to pick up. Are you still at work? You work too many hours, you know.'

'I'm at home.'

'Good. About time you saw that boyfriend or whatever you call him more often.'

Kay closed her eyes. 'Did you want something?'

'Yes. We're in France at the moment with Abby and the kids. Gorgeous weather. We're heading home tomorrow, so we'll call in to see you for dinner on the way back. You can fix us up with something, can't you?'

'Mum, I'm—'

'Fabulous. We'll see you then. Don't be late.'

Kay stared at the phone for a moment, stunned.

'What happened?' Adam pushed her refilled glass across the worktop to her.

'They're coming here. Tomorrow.'

'Your mum?'

'And my dad. And my sister. And the kids.'

'Why?'

'Apparently, they've been in France for the week. They're driving back tomorrow and want to call in for dinner.'

'Oh.'

Kay sank back on her bar stool and wrapped her

fingers around the stem of her glass. 'What am I going to do?'

Adam clasped her hand in his. 'You're going to put a brave face on it, try to get out of work at a reasonable time, and be a grown-up about it.'

Kay glared at him, then realised she was pouting. 'I'm not telling them tomorrow.'

'So, don't. You suffering a miscarriage last year is none of their business anyway. I'm not going to say anything. Don't worry about it – I'll sort out dinner tomorrow. If they're on their way back from France, your dad isn't going to want to stay long anyway.'

'You're right, I suppose.' She sighed, then checked her watch. 'It's getting on. What do you fancy to eat?'

A quirk began at the side of Adam's mouth.

'Don't.' She wagged a warning finger at him. 'I'm serious. I'm starving. What shall we have?'

'Let's be bad.'

She smiled. 'How bad?'

'Chinese takeaway.' He picked up his mobile phone and unplugged it from its charger, his thumb over the speed dial.

'That's not really bad. You lightweight.'

He rolled his eyes. 'Okay. Indian. From that place over near Spot Lane.'

'Now you're talking.'

'Woof,' said Holly.

CHAPTER EIGHT

The incident room continued to hum with an energy borne of a new investigation when Kay arrived the next morning.

Phones seemed to ring constantly, a mixture of landline calls and mobile, while admin staff dashed between the desks, distributing reports and dealing with requests for more research.

Sometimes, Kay envied Sharp the ability to be able to close his office door and block out some of the noise, although it was rare that he did so. He preferred to be involved at all times; happy to delegate, but always keeping a close watch on the progression of the case and the team's approach to it.

She dumped her bag under her desk and placed her coffee cup on top of a beer mat she'd acquired from the local pub on a night out with the team a few months ago. Barnes had persuaded her to try half a pint of the latest guest ale, and although she found it was an acquired taste and not one she was likely to attain, she'd loved the artwork for the pump clip and promotional material the brewery had provided to the pub. The landlord had handed her half a dozen of the cardboard squares, and she'd worked her way through them since, tossing them into the waste bin as they gradually fell apart over time.

Sharp stalked from his room, handed a stack of paperwork to one of the administrative assistants, and waved the team over.

'Tasks for today,' he said as they formed a semicircle opposite the whiteboard. 'We'll review the names we pulled from the list of suicides on railway tracks in the area yesterday, and research the circumstances. Before we do so, and in order that we don't assume that every single one is a murder victim, I'd like Sergeant Walker to provide some background information to you all regarding suicide statistics on railways.' He grimaced. 'Unfortunately, it's more common than any of us would like. Dave?'

'Thanks. I've put together a one-page summary for each of you, if you want to pass these around?' He waited a moment while the documents were shared out. 'For a start, over seventy-five per cent of all rail fatalities are suicides. Sadly, year on year, we're seeing an increase in overall numbers, and out of those suicides, eighty per cent are men.'

'Age range?' said Kay.

'Typically between thirty and fifty-five. These men

have often been unemployed for a long period of time, or in financial difficulties.'

'What's being done to try and stop them?' said Carys.

'There have been a lot of stations around here fitted with mid-platform fencing to stop people walking in front of express trains, and they've been spending money erecting cameras at popular suicide spots to alert staff,' he said. 'All of the station staff are trained in suicide prevention. They have a good success rate, too.'

Barnes took the handout Debbie passed to him and ran his eyes over the information. 'These stats say there are still over two hundred suicides on railways in the UK every year though.'

Walker shrugged. 'No system is perfect and, let's face it, if someone wants to kill themselves, they're going to find a way.'

'Okay, thanks, Dave,' said Sharp. 'Barnes? Give us a summary of yesterday's findings.'

'Looks as if things have gotten worse over the last six to twelve months,' said Barnes, and waved one of the reports. 'Some were prevented by railway staff – but then it's escalated.'

'Could be to do with the fact there's less funding for programmes to address mental health?' said Carys.

'Maybe,' said Sharp, taking the report from Barnes and scanning it. He glanced up at the whiteboard. 'Three of those eight people up there are within the past twelve months. The last one only two months ago. Have we got names for all of these, Ian?'

'Yeah. I've already drawn up a list of the relations and other contacts listed in the inquest reports for those three. I'll make some phone calls this morning and arrange for us to go and speak to them this afternoon or tomorrow, if you want?'

'That'd be good, thanks. What about background for them?'

'The first one, Stephen Taylor, was unemployed – his mother said he had a history of depression spanning two years before he jumped from a bridge into the path of a London-bound express train early one morning seven months ago. Nathan Cox died when he was hit by a train late one night over near Aylesford four months ago, and then there's the one from two months ago – Cameron Abbott. In and out of work as a labourer, apparently. Both Stephen and Cameron had been on antidepressants, and no one seemed surprised that they chose to end their lives.'

'What about doctors?'

'Different GPs. But, and this is something I'm going to follow up, both Stephen and Cameron had attended the same workshops organised by the local council after being found guilty and charged for drunk driving. Might be something there.'

'Let me know as soon as you find out anything. Work with Kay on that.'

'Will do.'

'Carys, can you work with Dave and get the inquest reports for the three suicides and speak to the investigating officers?' Sharp added the briefing notes to the whiteboard. 'I'll remind you to keep an open mind, ladies and gentlemen. If we have a killer on the loose who's done this before and got away with it, we need to stop him before he does it again.'

'You've got to admit, it's a perfect way to cover his tracks,' said Barnes, and then ducked as Gavin threw a soft stress ball at him while the others groaned in unison.

CHAPTER NINE

Kay hit "send" on the last email of her backlog, still fuming at Larch's attitude towards her the previous day, even though she knew he riled her on purpose.

Despite Sharp agreeing with her that two lines of enquiry would be prudent, it was obvious their DCI thought it was a complete waste of time.

She opened up a folder within her email inbox and scrolled through the text. Although several months old, it still managed to infuriate her.

Your application for the role of Detective Inspector has been unsuccessful at this time.

When she'd emailed back to enquire why, the HR team had been cagey, citing an oversubscribed application process. Kay had called foul on the response, stormed into Sharp's office and shut the door before demanding an explanation.

It was then that she had found out that Larch had

been responsible for having the ultimate word in her career ambitions.

It had been the final blow, and one that had dire consequences for her health – and that of the baby girl she'd only recently discovered she was carrying.

She had never understood Larch's animosity towards her. Since the last investigation where they had crossed paths, he had mostly ignored her – something for which she was grateful.

From time to time his name would crop up in a conversation and she would wonder where he was, almost tempted to check over her shoulder at times. For the past several months, he had been no more than a ghost. Often his whereabouts had been unknown, and when she had asked Sharp he had shrugged and denied all knowledge before making some excuse that the detective chief inspector was working on a special project for the chief superintendent. 'That's all I know about it, Kay. At least he's out of our way.'

She had been inclined to agree with him, and it was only now that he was involved in this latest investigation that she realised how much she had enjoyed not having him breathing down her neck. She glanced up as Barnes cleared his throat.

'Come on. Let's go grab some lunch. You look like you could use some fresh air.'

Twenty minutes later, standing in line at the pub counter to order their food, Kay peered across at her colleague and took in his new suit and tie.

He caught her staring at him. 'What?'

'New clothes?'

He cleared his throat. 'It was my daughter's idea. I've lost a bit of weight, and she said my old suit was looking a bit baggy.'

Kay raised an eyebrow. 'Losing weight and new clothes?' It struck her then that she hadn't seen Barnes having his usual takeaway lunches of burgers and chips since he'd returned to work. As it was, he'd just ordered a chicken salad. Her eyes narrowed. 'Are you seeing someone?'

'No.'

Kay said nothing more, grabbed her change and made her way across to the table where Carys and Gavin set.

As Barnes approached, Gavin gave a low wolf whistle. 'Looking quite suave there, Ian. Hadn't seen the new jacket this morning.'

Barnes glared at him, but Kay noted the sparkle of amusement in his eyes.

'Who's the lucky girl?' said Carys.

'There isn't a lucky girl. And mind your own business.'

Kay burst out laughing.

———

'This is what I was telling Sharp about,' said Barnes from the opposite desk after they'd returned from lunch.

He leaned over and pushed a printout across to Kay,

who was fighting a losing battle with the paperwork strewn across her workspace.

She glanced up, shook her head to clear her thoughts, and reached out for the page.

'This is the rehab programme?'

'Yeah,' he said, and moved around the desks to join her. 'Two of our suicide victims attended the same rehabilitation programme after being caught drink-driving,' he said, and stabbed at the page with his forefinger. 'Stephen Taylor and Cameron Abbott. Each of them lost their driving licence for a period of six months, and a condition of their sentence was to attend a weekly rehabilitation session about the dangers of drink driving for a period of four weeks.'

'Who else was on the programme at the same time?'

'Four others. I've made arrangements for Carys to go and speak with them later this morning with Gavin, if we talk to the families of the suicide victims.'

'Sounds like a plan. You hear Gavin's studying for his detective exams?'

'Yeah. Carys mentioned it. Didn't seem too happy.'

'I think our golden child might be getting a bit anxious about some competition in the team.' Kay smiled and lowered her voice. 'I've been making a point of trying to split the caseloads equally between them, so they can't accuse me of favouritism.'

Barnes chuckled. 'That bad?'

'No, not really, and I can see it from her point of view. But Sharp isn't taking sides, so nor should we.'

'Interesting dynamic.'

53

'It is.' Kay lowered her gaze back to the document in her hand. 'What were the circumstances for our victims being on this rehabilitation programme in the first place?'

'Taylor was doing a few miles an hour over the speed limit on the A20 near The Landway – his car was caught by a speed trap, and when the officers pulled him over and breathalysed him, he was caught driving drunk as well. The magistrate took into account the fact that he was taking antidepressants at the time, but if he was on those he shouldn't have been drinking in the first place, so she confiscated his licence and put him on the programme.'

'Any previous history?'

'None at all. The only other information I've been able to find out is from the court records. Taylor was unemployed at the time, and had been for a few months. Looks like he was in and out of work before that.'

'What about our second victim?'

'Cameron Abbott was spotted by a uniform patrol in the centre of Maidstone. He came out of a pub on the High Street, wobbled his way down to The Mall car park, and got into his car. They arrested him as soon as he turned the key in the ignition. Apparently, it was a first time offence, and he was contrite enough that the magistrate slapped him with a fine and a six month ban, plus the rehabilitation programme. Again, no prior record.'

Kay handed back the printout of the names. 'What did the rehabilitation programme entail?'

'Group discussions, safety videos, things like that. They try to re-educate offenders about the dangers of drunk driving, in the hope they won't reoffend once they get their licence back.'

'Good success rate?'

'Seems to be, although whether that's down to the rehabilitation programme, or people not wanting to risk all the hassle of losing their driving licence again can't be proven.'

'Who runs it?'

'It's outsourced to a company called "Mending Ways". Basically, a couple of psychologists teamed up and pitched the idea. They've been running it for a year and a half at the community hall in Shepway.'

'Anyone spoken to them yet?'

'Not yet – do you want it?'

'Yeah. Give me the number. I'll give them a call and see if we can drop by to see them before speaking to the families.'

CHAPTER TEN

Kay steered the car around the roundabout, and took the second exit. The road ran alongside the back of a school, and soon the community hall appeared on the left-hand side.

Half a dozen cars filled the parking spaces outside the low-set building, and Kay pulled into one of the spare spaces.

'My daughter used to come here for karate lessons when she was little,' said Barnes. 'I can't believe it's still here.'

'Good job it is. I don't think some of these groups would have anywhere else to meet otherwise.'

Kay led the way into the hall's entrance through a set of double doors, and was immediately struck by the distinct smell of sweaty training shoes. She wrinkled her nose and peered around the small atrium. Two sets of doors faced her, both of which were shut. She checked her watch.

'According to the website, they have a session running at the moment that should be finished in the next couple of minutes,' she said, 'so we shouldn't have long to wait.'

They paced the entrance hall, and Kay ran her eyes over the various community notices pinned to a cork board that ran the length of the wall. She turned as one of the doors opened, and a small group of people began to file out past her and Barnes, heading towards the car park.

She gave it another minute to allow for any stragglers, and then led Barnes through the door and into the hall.

The smooth surface of the floor had borne the brunt of various indoor sports over the years, its shiny surface pitted and scratched in places. Kay hovered at the threshold, unsure whether she should walk on the surface in her heels. As she was debating whether to proceed, one of two men remaining in the room saw her hesitate, and called out.

'You must be the detective I spoke to on the phone. Come on over – this floor has seen plenty of wear and tear. One more pair of shoes won't hurt it.'

Kay couldn't help but smile and led Barnes across the room where the two men were stacking the chairs from the session and placing them against the far wall out of the way. They turned as Kay and Barnes approached, and the man who had spoken held out his hand.

'I'm Malcolm Bannister. You must be Detective

Sergeant Kay Hunter?'

'That's right. And this is my colleague, Detective Constable Ian Barnes. Thanks for taking the time to speak with us this morning.'

The man shook Barnes's hand and gestured to his colleague. 'This is Ethan Aspley. He helps me with the sessions for our drink driving cases.'

'It echoes a bit too much in here,' said Aspley. 'There's a small office on the mezzanine level. Why don't we go and use that instead? It's more private, too.'

'Sounds good,' said Kay. 'Lead the way.'

She and Barnes followed the two men out of the hall and up a short flight of stairs onto a low mezzanine floor. Open plan, it consisted of a couple of desks in the middle of the room, filing cabinets labelled with the name of each club that used the hall, and an array of sporting equipment in various states of disrepair.

She waited until they'd pulled out chairs and Barnes had extracted his notebook from the inside of his jacket. 'How long has this programme been running?'

'Just over two years now. We first pitched the idea to the council three years ago, but it took nearly seven months for them to implement it. Something about budget management and the new financial year at the time.'

'Whose idea was it?'

'We'd both been practising psychology for a number of years,' said Bannister. 'Then, my sister was killed by a man who was later found to be three times over the limit. I remember seeing the man's family at the magistrates' court. It seemed such a waste. He was happily married, had a really good job, and had thrown it all away because he'd had too many drinks before getting in his car. It preyed on my mind for months, and then Ethan here mentioned that perhaps we could do something in my sister's memory, and that's when we came up with the idea for this programme.'

'If it was my sister that had been killed, I don't know if I could have envisaged doing something as noble as this.'

A faint smile crossed his lips. 'It hasn't been easy, Detective, I'll grant you that. But we have a good success rate, and it's rare that attendees reoffend.'

'What about you, Ethan? What was your interest in starting this up?'

'I was engaged to Malcolm's sister. He was falling apart and so was I, to be honest. We both needed something to focus on.'

'Tell me about when Stephen Taylor and Cameron Abbott killed themselves. When did you find out?'

Bannister ran a hand through his hair. 'It was a shock, that's for sure. I mean, we address the issue of the drink driving offence, and we do take into consideration any other issues a client might be having. But to find out that two men have chosen to end their lives only months after leaving us? I had no idea. When I heard through the newspapers, I spent hours wracking my brains trying to recall whether either of them gave any indication they would do something like that. I couldn't.'

'Do you keep in touch with people, once they leave the programme?'

'No. We provide them with the support they need during the rehabilitation period. Once they leave here, that's it – although we do provide them with contact details for places like Alcoholics Anonymous, and we encourage them to speak with their GPs if we believe there are underlying issues that ought to be discussed.'

'And you never saw Stephen Taylor or Cameron Abbott again?'

'No. Never.'

Kay turned to Aspley, but he shook his head.

'Me neither.'

Kay rose from her chair. 'In that case, gentlemen, I think we're done here. Thank you for your time.'

Barnes tossed the car keys to her as they left the building. 'I want to add some more to my notes while you drive.'

'You'll do the usual checks about them? Professional record, any previous convictions and the like?'

'Yes. That'd already crossed my mind listening to the pair of them.'

'What do you think? Too good to be true?'

'If it was my sister or fiancée that was killed, I'd be a damn sight more angry than those two.'

'A commendable way of dealing with grief, though.'

'It'd be easier to move a body onto railway tracks if there were two of you.'

'Now there's a cheerful thought.'

CHAPTER ELEVEN

Kay pushed open the car door and waited for Barnes while she cast her eyes over the house in front of her.

A path led directly across a grass verge from the kerb to the front door of what had once been Stephen Taylor's home. A fence had been erected to the left of the house with a locked gate that Kay presumed went through to the garden, while a wheelie bin stood on the outside of it, a cluster of bluebottle flies buzzing around the lid. Underneath the front window, a variety of large pots contained a half-hearted attempt at gardening. A single ornamental lamp hung above the front door, which was sheltered from the elements by a protruding porch.

She pressed the bell, then turned and faced the street as she waited for the door to be opened.

Beyond the garden wall were two narrow lines of terraced houses. Each property had the same outlook – a red brick frontage, a front door in the same style – apart from one or two rebellious neighbours who had installed bespoke designs – and a front window, with two upper windows overlooking the street below.

Some properties – Kay supposed, owned by more elderly people – had some care taken about them. The others looked a little more rundown; three doors up on the opposite side, a car sat on bricks, its paintwork rusting and cobwebs in the windscreen. She guessed it hadn't moved for at least six months.

'Nice neighbourhood,' said Barnes. 'Are these all council owned?'

Kay wrinkled her nose. 'Actually, I think all these are privately owned,' she said. She turned at the sound of somebody approaching the door.

It opened, and a woman who Kay guessed to be in her late fifties peered out.

'What do you want?'

Kay introduced themselves. 'Would you mind if we came in, Mrs Taylor?'

The woman's upper lip curled, but she stepped aside and held open the door.

Her eyes travelled over Kay and then Barnes as they stepped inside before she wiped at sleepy eyes.

'What's this about? David's not in trouble again is he?'

Kay waited until the door shut, and glanced at Barnes before speaking. 'Who's David?'

'He's me son. What's he done now?'

Kay shook her head. 'We're not here about David,' she said. 'We'd like to speak with you about Stephen.'

The woman took a step back and frowned. 'Stephen?'

'Can we sit down somewhere?'

The woman nodded, her brow still creased, and led the way past a flight of stairs, down a narrow hallway and through to a kitchen that looked as if it hadn't left the 1980s.

'Do you want a cup of tea?'

Kay took one look at the greasy surfaces and the overflowing pedal bin, and thought better of it. 'No, thanks, we won't take up too much of your time.'

'Fine.' The woman gestured to the sparse kitchen table and the four chairs gathered around it. 'Sit yourselves down. What you want to know?'

'First of all, I must ask that this conversation isn't repeated to anyone else at this time,' said Kay. 'We're currently investigating a suspicious death on the railway line between East Malling and Barming.'

The woman rocked back in her chair, her eyebrows raised. 'Another suicide?'

'That's what we're trying to establish,' said Kay. 'I'm sorry, I know Stephen died seven months ago, but it would help our investigation if you could tell me what happened, and what his state of mind was before he died.'

'State of mind? I'll tell you what his state of mind was. It was all over the place. He hadn't worked for months, not after losing his job. It was the final straw after being caught drink driving. We nearly lost the house because he couldn't pay the rent. I gave up asking when he would get another job, so I ended up leaving him at home so there was someone here when the kids got back from school in the afternoons, and I went and worked at the local supermarket stocking shelves from three o'clock to nine at night.'

'How did he lose his job?'

The woman shrugged. 'He was suffering from depression,' she said. 'And, as usual, his bosses didn't understand. It was really hard for him to explain that sometimes he just couldn't get out of bed. He wasn't lazy. He'd just have this melancholy that was sucking him under and he'd be lost for days.'

She pushed herself out of her chair, and wandered across to the sink before gazing out the window at the simple garden. 'If I'm honest, I always knew he'd kill himself.' She turned back to face Kay, tears glistening at the corners of her eyes. 'I didn't know how to stop him, though. He tried, he really did – even went to the doctor and got prescribed some pills to take, but it was too late. They didn't work in time. Afterwards, at the inquest, the doctor said the antidepressants would have kicked in within another couple of weeks.' She sniffed. 'Stephen might've been okay after that.'

'I understand he attended a rehabilitation programme after a drink driving offence. Can you tell me anything about that?'

'Well, it didn't do him any good, did it?' She shook her head. 'It made things worse, to be honest. He felt so bad about being caught drink driving, although I think that was more embarrassment than anything else. He couldn't wait to complete the programme and get his licence back.'

Kay leaned forward. 'Can you recall any friends he might have spoken to in the days leading up to his death?'

The woman snorted. 'All his friends fell by the wayside. He'd get a call occasionally, or a text message – I suppose one of them would try to get him out for a drink or something, get him out of the house – but he'd always turn it down. In the end, they stopped phoning him.'

'Do you have any idea what might have caused his depression to worsen?'

'Losing that last job was the final straw. He'd been out of work for two months prior to starting there but like I said, they didn't understand about his moods and after a written warning, they fired him.'

She wiped at her eyes, and Kay gestured to Barnes that they would leave.

'Mrs Taylor, thank you for talking with us today,' she said, and handed over one of her cards. 'If you think of anything unusual that might have happened leading up to Stephen's death, or recall anyone phoning him prior to that day, would you let me know?'

'You think someone drove him to suicide?'

Kay pursed her lips. 'No, no I don't. Not at this time,' she said. 'We're simply making sure we don't overlook anything in relation to our current investigation.'

CHAPTER TWELVE

Cameron Abbott's house provided a completely different aspect from the first one that they had visited.

Two cars took up the limited amount of space on the narrow concrete driveway below the house, and a dry stone block wall faced the road with two red brick pillars set each side of a short flight of steps that led to the front door. The end of terrace residence had been rendered to disguise its original pebble-dashed finish although the bumpy surface remained, while the small front garden contained a variety of shrubs; here and there a few early daffodils poked out from beneath the other plants, overlooked by a large bay window.

Barnes pressed the doorbell and a soft chime sounded from within.

A few moments later a shadow appeared beyond the frosted glass panel at the top of the door. It opened, and a woman peered out at them, pushing short blonde hair out of her eyes. Wearing black leggings and a cream silk shirt, her appearance was preceded by a waft of musk-based perfume.

'Good morning. Denise Abbott?' said Kay. She introduced herself and Barnes. 'May we come in, please?'

The woman blinked, and then stepped to one side.

'Of course,' she said.

She closed the front door, and turned to face them. She crossed her arms over her chest. 'Is this about the suicide that happened the other day?'

'Yes,' said Kay, 'That's right.'

The woman shrugged. 'Not sure what I can do to help you. You're obviously here because my husband killed himself on the same stretch of track two months ago. It doesn't sound like the railway has done anything to prevent people from doing that since.'

Close up, the woman appeared older and Kay noticed flecks of grey amongst her blonde hair. Large rings covered the majority of her fingers, and she gestured with her hands constantly.

Kay suspected it was an attempt to show off the jewellery.

She realised that the woman was eager to get rid of them. 'If you wouldn't mind, could you tell me what your husband's state of mind was leading up to his suicide? Did you have any indication that he might do something so drastic?'

'He was always depressed. Even before he lost his job. He was just one of those people that never seemed happy. We'd be on holiday somewhere like the south of

France, and he'd still find something to be miserable about.'

Kay counted to five in her head before proceeding. 'In the weeks leading up to his death, did he seem worried about anything in particular?'

'Not really. Not that I recall.'

A floorboard creaked above their heads.

Kay arched her eyebrow, but said nothing.

The woman looked annoyed. 'My partner, Vince. I hope you're not going to look down your nose and tell me I should be acting like the grieving widow.'

'None of my business,' said Kay. 'You were saying about your husband's state of mind?'

The woman sighed. 'The doctor gave him antidepressants. They tried a small dose at first, but it wouldn't work. You have to wait a few weeks for them to kick in. When that didn't work, the doctor prescribed a stronger dosage. He didn't have any work at the time, and the drugs made him lethargic. He just sat around the house all day, watching television or staring into space.'

'I understand that he was admitted to a rehabilitation programme for drink driving offenders?'

'Stupid thing to do. He was driving his brother's car at the time, too and he wasn't impressed, I can tell you. Waste of time, as well. Didn't help him, did it?'

'What about his friends?'

'What about them? They tried phoning of course, when his depression started to get worse, but after a while they got tired of trying to get him out of the house. If they did go for a drink or were going on a

fishing trip, he would just make it worse for all of them.'
She shrugged. 'They stopped calling him in the end.'

'Do you know if he met anyone, that day?'

Abbott's widow shook her head. 'Like I said, a lot of
his old work colleagues and friends drifted away once
the depression got worse.' Her hands shook as she
dabbed her eyes once more. 'There was hardly anyone
at his funeral.'

'Would you be able to let us have a note of his
friends and work colleagues' names – and phone
numbers, if you still have them?'

'Of course. I have an address book somewhere.
Hang on.'

She left the kitchen, and Kay heard her move along
the hallway, to where she presumed an address book
would be kept next to the landline phone she'd spotted
on a small cabinet next to the front door.

She returned after a few minutes, and held out a
black leather book to Kay. 'It's probably easier if you
take this and photocopy it, isn't it?'

'Yes, if you're sure?'

The woman nodded. 'I've put an asterisk next to the
names of people you might want to talk to.'

Kay took the book from her. 'Thank you. I'll have
the details noted down as soon as we return to the
station, and I'll return it as soon as possible.'

As Kay and Barnes walked back to the car, she
paused to stand on the pavement and stare at the house.

'What are you thinking?'

'Both Stephen Taylor and Cameron Abbott had lost

all contact with their friends before they died. Effectively, they were isolated. What if that made them more vulnerable to a killer?'

'Let's not jump to conclusions, Kay. Isolation is a big factor in depression – people don't understand it, so they don't know how to deal with it if a friend suffers from it.'

She sighed. 'I know. It's just a thought.'

'I'll keep it in mind.'

He ran his hand over the page in front of him, leaned over and gently blew across its surface.

The eraser moved back and forth, the soft grey graphite disappearing under its force until the lines he'd drawn over the past hour had completely disappeared.

A plate of cheese and biscuits rested near his elbow. A fly paused on a corner of the plate, flexed its wings, then took off again.

He flapped his hand next to his ear as it drew too close, and tried to concentrate.

In the corner of the room, an old model flat screen television flickered as a series of advertisements finished, and a programme returned to the screen. The presenter was walking in front of a large factory, gesticulating to the camera while trying to appear nonchalantly informative at the same time. The scene changed to one of inside the factory, huge robotic arms turning panels of sheet metal into cars.

He snorted derisively at the presenter's turn of phrase, then reached out for the remote control next to him and pressed the "mute" button.

He couldn't afford the distraction, not after last time.

Besides, he knew the episode; had watched all of them over and over again.

It helped to pass the time, once.

He leaned back and gazed around the room.

Net curtains covered the window, while dust motes floated in the air, dancing in the muted light.

He tried to recall the last time he'd cleaned the place.

He frowned, his eyes taking in the thin layer of dust that covered everything, and wondered if he should make an effort to do something about it.

He preferred to work in the garden, if he was honest. Of course, that meant he had to exchange pleasantries with his nosy next door neighbour, or with the young couple that lived in the adjacent house, but if the garden was tidy, they left him alone. No one knew that the inside of the building bore little resemblance to the tidiness and order of the exterior.

It wasn't as if he invited people in for a cup of tea, after all.

No, the cleaning could wait. He had more important things to do.

His eyes fell back to the table before him. A mobile phone lay silent at the far end, a lead snaking out from it to the power point on the far wall.

It didn't ring much; everyone had given up calling

him after the first few months, and he had no intention of calling anyone.

He liked the games, though. Simple ones, like solitaire or Sudoku. Games he could lose hours playing, while he thought of everything and nothing.

He dropped the eraser, pushed away the highlighter pens and calculator, then picked up the map once more. He shuffled, trying to ease the tension in his spine. He'd been hunched over for too long, lost to time, too busy concentrating on the job in hand.

For that's what it was.

A job.

A project. Defined as a scope of work with a finite end.

Everything had been on schedule until two nights ago.

He fought down the anger.

He hadn't seen the dog walker before, so she hadn't been factored into his plans.

Luckily, she'd been on the other side of the tracks to him, and the beam from her torch was too weak to pick him out as he'd crouched next to his victim, listening.

The dog had seen him though, he was sure.

The woman had been too busy trying to find a way to break down the wire mesh fencing, but the dog had heard him as he'd begun to slink away from his position and into the shadows, and had started to bark once more.

He'd only gone a few paces.

It had been different this time.

The others hadn't been conscious when they'd died. Somehow, at the time, he thought it would be easier to deal with, but there was something missing – he didn't feel anything afterwards.

No sense of accomplishment.

No sense that he'd contributed to setting everything back on its proper axis.

When this one had woken from his slumber to find his hands and feet tied to the tracks, his terror had been palpable.

Groggy at first, he had squirmed and bucked as an express train had torn past him on the opposite track.

And that's when he'd decided to stay.

He wanted to see, wanted to hear the man's terror as the train bore down on him.

It had worked.

The moment the train had screeched to a halt only a short distance from where he stood, he'd exhaled and the tension he'd been holding between his neck and shoulders dissipated a little.

The headaches had returned within hours, as they always did, but the sense of equilibrium had remained.

His eyes fell to the notebook.

He had to concentrate.

There was plenty of work to do yet and now the police were involved, his schedule had changed.

Accelerated.

But that was the thing with projects, wasn't it? Once the job was done, you took stock, conducted an assessment, and made sure that all those risks that had nearly put an end to your carefully laid plans were accounted for next time.

Mitigated, so the next attempt was perfected.

His eyes travelled over the calculations he'd written down in his notebook and then he smiled, leaned forward and picked up the pencil once more, the nib hovering over the map laid out before him.

He had another project to deliver on schedule.

CHAPTER FOURTEEN

Kay's heart sank a little as she turned into her street and noticed the two extra cars parked outside at the kerb.

She knew she'd have to expect a visit from her family soon, and she suspected the fact her mother had suggested that they drop by on their way home from a holiday in France with her sister and young family meant she was only doing so out of a misplaced sense of duty.

They'd never been close, and as Kay had continued to rise through the ranks in the police, they had drifted even further apart.

Aside from the occasional phone call from either of them, she preferred to keep her distance; her mother was too overbearing, and her sister drove her to distraction.

Having them turn up at short notice set her teeth on edge – before she'd even turned off the ignition.

She glanced down as her phone began to vibrate, and recognised Adam's mobile number.

'Hello?'

'You can't sit out there forever, you know.' His teasing tone took the edge off her nerves a little.

'I could drive off and leave you there all alone with them.'

'Ohh, nasty.' He chuckled. 'It's not all that bad. Your dad's here, too.'

'Don't worry, I'm on my way in.'

Kay ended the call and slipped her phone into her bag before climbing from the car and locking it, then took a deep breath and slouched towards the house.

She'd never told her parents or her sister about the miscarriage she'd suffered the previous year.

She didn't want their sympathy, and it would have provided her mother with another excuse to berate her for putting her career first, instead of marrying Adam and starting a family.

Her mother possessed little tact, and had no consideration for what her older daughter might want from her life, let alone what Adam thought. Instead, she spent every moment of their irregular phone conversations telling Kay what she should be doing with her life.

Nothing had changed since Kay had been a teenager, and from the moment she'd been able to leave home to go to university, she'd continued to put as much distance between her and her family as possible.

She took a deep breath and inserted her key into the front door lock and tried to push it open as quietly as possible.

The moment she stepped over the threshold, the grating tone of her sister's voice reached her, and she exhaled.

She checked her watch and made a quick calculation. From the aromas, Adam already had dinner ready to go, so with any luck they'd be gone within a couple of hours as her dad didn't like to drive late at night, and they still had a long journey to get home.

Voices carried from the living area, her mother's compensating for the lack of interaction from anyone else, already scolding the oldest child for failing to complete a colouring book properly.

Kay rolled her eyes and dashed upstairs, shedding her work clothes and pulling on jeans and a fresh shirt before checking her make-up in the mirror and pulling a brush through her hair.

There was no point in giving her mother an easy target.

She sighed and headed downstairs, pushing through the door to the living room and cutting off her mother's harsh tones mid-sentence.

'There she is.'

The words hit Kay in the solar plexus, all her childhood memories flooding back. She clenched her fists at her sides, her fingernails digging into her palms, and forced a smile.

'Hi, everyone.'

'Hello, love,' her father said, standing up from his place in Adam's favourite armchair and pulling her into a hug.

She returned the embrace, and noticed that despite his advancing years, he still had a full head of thick silver hair and the enthusiasm of a teenager.

'How was France?'

'Lovely, thanks. You're looking well.'

'She looks thin,' her mother snapped. She rose regally from the sofa and handed the baby to Kay's sister in one fluid motion, and then stalked across the room and presented her cheek.

In contrast to her husband, her face appeared pinched, her make-up too heavy and her hair colour three shades too dark for her complexion.

Kay gave her a quick kiss, and resisted the urge to wipe her mouth afterwards.

She turned at movement behind her as Adam appeared, a rueful smile on his face. 'Hello.'

'Hi. Dinner's nearly ready, if you all want to come through?'

After a quick greeting to her sister and a playful tug of her elder niece's ponytail, Kay traipsed into the kitchen after her family and waited while her mother fussed around getting everyone seated around the central worktop.

'Why you two can't buy a dining table like everyone else, I don't know,' she said, tutting loud enough to make Holly raise her head from her bed. 'It's impossible to sit comfortably on these bar stool things.'

Kay bit back the retort that formed on her lips and instead busied herself with taking plates from cupboards, handing out cutlery and topping up her mother and sister's wine glasses.

Her father joined her, helping himself to a soft drink from the fridge, and winked at her.

'Didn't Silas join you in France?' she asked her sister.

'Too busy.' Abby shrugged. 'There's a big merger going on at work at the moment. He was hoping to fly down to join us, but they wanted him to go to Aberdeen at the last minute.'

'That's a shame.'

Her sister forced a smile. 'It's okay. We'll have a proper family holiday in the summer.' She leaned across and took the toddler from her mother's grasp and placed her on her knee to feed her. 'At least it gave Mum and Dad a chance to catch up with these two.'

'They're growing so fast.'

'It's because you never see them,' said her mother. 'Look at what time you got home tonight.'

'We're in the middle of a murder investigation—'

'Not in front of the kids,' her sister hissed, and glared at her.

'Why don't you find something nice to do?' her mother continued. 'You've got a good degree. You could have your pick of any job out there. One that'll mean you have a life outside of work, too.'

Kay put down her fork and took a large sip of wine, counting to ten as she did so.

An hour and a half later, and her ordeal was almost over. Her sister sat in the living room, the two kids beginning to grow sleepy, and her mother informed them they would be leaving shortly to begin the final leg of their journey home.

Kay managed to stop herself from sighing out loud with relief, and then nearly choked on the last of her wine as Adam fist-pumped the air behind her mother's back.

Her father had his hands in the kitchen sink, busy with the washing up, and Kay grabbed a tea towel and began to dry the pots and pans while Adam took a tray laden with coffee mugs through to the others.

'What's wrong, love?' her father said.

'What do you mean?'

He glanced sideways at her. 'You always were rotten at keeping secrets.'

She sighed. 'It's nothing, Dad, really.'

'I know your mother's always going on about you having a career instead of kids,' he said, 'but it's your life. You and Adam do what's best for you. Take no notice of her.'

He stopped, leaned across, and picked up the other tea towel before drying his hands, his eyes never leaving hers. 'I know something's troubling you, and I don't mean your mother nagging you all the time. If you ever need to talk, you phone me, okay?' A small smile quirked at his lips. 'Best make it a Tuesday, though. That's when your mother goes to bingo.'

Kay blinked back tears, and closed the gap between them.

'Thanks, Dad.'

CHAPTER FIFTEEN

Peter Bailey tugged the collar of his jacket up and shoved his hands into his pockets.

His shift had ended twenty minutes ago, and he normally endured a fifty-minute walk between the supermarket and the flat he rented. The crisp evening air nipped at his skin, and he picked up his pace to try and keep warm.

Things were looking up at work. He'd only been there for six weeks, but the manager of the store had pulled him to one side earlier that day and asked if he would be interested in a couple more hours every day.

He agreed without hesitation. The extra money would mean he could start saving and, by the end of the year, he might even have enough to treat himself to a cheap holiday.

The thought put a bounce in his step.

On his doctor's orders, he had started to reduce the dosage of his prescription tablets. The doctor had been wary at first, and had cautioned him about the side effects.

He shook his head a little. They had had a similar conversation when he had first been prescribed the antidepressants. Except now, he could begin to lose weight with any luck. He had always taken care of his health before, but after the accident one thing had led to the other and it had become easier to rely on takeaway food and soft drinks. He only had himself to blame, and he realised that at the time he had sought comfort in the food. With the extra money he'd be earning the following week, he'd be able to join the local gym.

He withdrew his right hand from his pocket and slapped the button for the pedestrian crossing. As he watched the cars and buses race past, his mind wandered and he found himself planning how his daily routine would change once his new shifts began the next week.

A lorry braked in front of him and the driver beeped the horn.

He blinked, and realised the green man icon was shining from the opposite side of the road. He held up a hand to the truck driver, and hurried across the black and white stripes of the crossing, reaching the other side as the lights began to flash.

A cool breeze whipped at his hair as he made his way across the bridge over the river. It had seemed ages since he had a night out, and a couple of swift halves at a pub that was once a favourite haunt had made a refreshing change on the way home from work. He'd certainly been gasping for a beer since being on the antidepressants, and the moment his doctor had cagily agreed he could have the occasional drink, he'd made plans to rectify that thirst as soon as possible.

There hadn't been much happening in the pub when he got there, for which he was grateful. He still struggled to interact socially, something his counsellor had said was perfectly normal and also that he shouldn't rush himself into social situations but rather take it slowly. Instead, he had sipped at his beer, kept his eye on the football score on the television in the far corner, and let the voices around him wash over his weary body.

He peered over the edge of the parapet into the dark waters of the Medway River below, his eyes tracing the silhouetted outline of the barges and other vessels moored to one side. He envied the freedom he envisaged their owners had; being able to unhitch a rope and drift along with the water's currents until another location took their fancy. He sniffed the damp air before picking up his pace and following the direction of the Tonbridge Road.

He checked over his shoulder. The road behind him was empty, and no one else was in sight. At the end of the road, traffic from the town centre sped past the junction, but no vehicles slowed to enter the estate.

Turning right into the road that would eventually lead to where he lived, the hairs on the back of his neck stood on end, and he paused.

The shunt and clang of a passing train reached his

ears, and his skin prickled with goose bumps. He forced himself to whistle, to take his mind off the distant sounds. His whistling was tuneless, but his heart rate began to decrease as the noise of the train faded.

He turned left before the Barracks railway station and picked up his pace.

He frowned. He had reduced the dose of his tablets a week ago, and apart from a slight dizziness if he stood too quickly, he hadn't noticed the side effects the doctor had warned him about. He wondered if paranoia was one the doctor had overlooked.

He spun on his heel, and as he passed under the next street light, he flicked the sleeve of his jacket back and checked his watch. It was nine-fifteen, and most of the houses he passed were in darkness, the inhabitants hidden behind closed blinds and curtains.

The street was deserted.

Or was it?

He glanced over his shoulder once more, and then stumbled. Resolving to watch where he stepped, he reached a T-junction and jogged across the road.

The sensation of being watched wouldn't leave him, though. He clenched his fists by his sides, his senses alert. He couldn't hear footsteps over the sound of distant traffic; yet he couldn't shake the sensation that he was under surveillance. Instead, he picked up his pace and ran the last few metres to the main doors to the block of flats.

The wide and cracked pavement gave way to a steep narrow grass verge that led down towards the ground floor of the flats. A concrete bridge with railings each side spanned the distance between the pavement and the building, and finished at a wide front door that was used by all the residents.

The flats on the lower floor were accessed by a flight of descending stairs from the entrance hall. Peter ignored these, and jogged up the stairs to his third-floor flat.

He took the stairs two at a time and, not caring what the neighbours thought if they happened to open their front door, he ran the length of the passageway to his front door.

By the time he reached it, sweat poured down his face. He wiped his sleeve across his forehead and extracted his keys from the pocket of his jeans. His hand shook as he inserted the key and he swore under his breath while he tried to twist and turn it. Eventually, the door opened and he slipped inside, slamming it behind him and making sure the locking mechanism slid back into place.

He leaned against the door, panting, then spun around and jammed the security chain across for good measure.

After a few moments, he shrugged himself out of his jacket and hung it up on the hook next to the door, and then padded along the hallway to the living area. He ignored the light switches. Enough ambient light from the glass panel above his front door shone through to the living room so he could navigate the furniture without tripping over or stubbing a toe. He lowered himself to his hands and knees and crawled towards the front window and then raised himself up until he was able to peer over the sill. The street outside was deserted except for a lone cat that darted between two parked cars.

He sat for a moment before he pushed himself to his feet, and pulled the curtains. He reached out and switched on the small lamp on the table next to him, and then made his way through to the kitchen.

Flicking the kettle on, he reached across the worktop for the plastic bottle next to the kitchen knives, uncapped it, and tipped out his daily dose.

His eyes rested on the collection of pills in his palm.

Peter's thoughts returned to the paranoia that had seized him walking home from the town, and he tipped two of the tablets back into the bottle.

'The sooner I'm off these, the better.'

CHAPTER SIXTEEN

He strode beside the worn access road, the surface churned up by the number of work vehicles that had been travelling up and down it for the past two weeks.

He'd parked a quarter of a mile away. He could have got closer if he wanted to in the car, but it was easier this way. He didn't want his vehicle to be seen so near to the railway tracks.

The air held a bite to it, a freshness only a few degrees away from a morning frost. He inhaled the earthy scent of the mud track beside him, careful to keep to the grass verge so he didn't leave a trail of footprints.

His progress was camouflaged by a high bramble hedgerow that separated the track from a fallow field intersected by a public footpath. At the weekend, the route would be busy with various walking groups all making their way to the pub in the nearby village.

He'd been watching the work crew for the past week. He knew they arrived before eight o'clock, so that they would be in time for the daily safety briefing. He knew that there were six of them, a mix of ages, all men.

He had even caught the train from Maidstone to Kemsing so that he could travel along the section of track the maintenance work was being carried out on.

He had seen then how he could reach his chosen location.

It was perfect.

He soon reached the temporary gates and fencing that had been placed across the access road. He drew closer and reached out to touch the thick chain looped around the gates to hold them secure, a large padlock holding it together.

A faint smile crossed his lips.

He withdrew a strange-looking key from his pocket, and inserted it into the padlock.

It turned smoothly.

The site was deserted – he had at least another hour before anybody else would turn up. The wind lifted his hair as he ran his eyes over the three temporary project offices that had been set up for the crew's use. Over towards the back of the small site two temporary toilets had been set up, the bright blue telephone box-like structures a little out of place in the otherwise bland landscape.

Abandoned plant machinery had been parked to one side a little way inside the fence – far enough away that kids wouldn't be tempted to enter the enclosure to reach them. A huge pyramid of grey ballast had been dumped to his right side, and steel rails were piled up next to it.

A small rise towards the back of the site led up to the railway track.

He hung back, his ears detecting the tell-tale sound of a train approaching.

He moved so he was hidden behind one of the temporary project offices, moments before the train flew past, its horn sounding in its wake.

He waited for a few moments, to make sure no other trains were about to pass.

Although he knew the train timetables by rote, there was always the risk a locomotive might be shunting between stations in amongst the passenger trains.

Satisfied that he wouldn't be observed until the next train was due to pass in twenty minutes, he made his way over to the fence separating the work site and the track. It had been cut and moved to one side by the maintenance workers. The temporary fencing that he had unlocked was designed to prevent the public from accessing the railway line.

He crossed the tracks to a rough grass verge that hugged the wayside and led down to a copse of trees that sheltered the site from view.

He grunted, and his shoulders relaxed a little. It was better than he had hoped.

Beyond the field the nearest houses were another half a mile away. He knew this because he had driven down the road observing the perfect gardens and the rolling landscape around them.

He also knew from his observations that the occupants of the three houses nearest to the field overlooking the railway would be at work when he returned.

There was only one problem with having a house in such an idyllic location. The size of a typical mortgage meant an early morning commute to a job in the city, and a late return home in the evening.

There would be no one to observe him.

He turned away from the houses, and made his way back over the tracks. He stopped between the two sets of rails, his steel-capped boots sinking a little into the uneven surface.

He lifted his head and gazed towards the horizon, the rails disappearing under a footbridge a good half a mile away. The footbridge was deserted, the call of a blackbird the only sound breaking the silence. A shiver ran down his spine.

It would be so easy to wait for the next train. There were only a few minutes until it was due to arrive, and it wouldn't slow down. He could simply walk out in front of it at the last minute, and the driver wouldn't be able to do anything about it.

Or, if he shifted a little to his right, his boot would touch the live rail and he'd be electrocuted in an instant.

He blinked, and forced the temptation from his mind.

He wouldn't end it, not until the project was complete.

He had a target, and he intended to meet it.

CHAPTER SEVENTEEN

The desk phone next to Kay's elbow rang, and she reached out for it while pushing a pile of paperwork to one side.

'Hello?'

'Results are in for the tyre treads,' said Harriet. 'You're not going to like it.'

'Hit me with it.'

'They're a cheap brand, same as used by a tyre repair and replacement parts franchise up and down the country. Usually fitted to one of the smaller car models. No distinguishing marks, normal wear and tear.'

'Crap.'

'I hear you.'

'Sorry, Harriet – I realise you're doing your best with what you've got.'

'No problem. I hate mysteries, too. I have got something of interest for you, though. When we were analysing what was left of the rope around the victim's ankle, we found a fingernail embedded in the fibres. At first, we thought it belonged to our victim, but it doesn't match his DNA. So—'

'It belongs to his killer.'

'Exactly. I'll email over my full report within the next twenty minutes, but I thought you might want to know now to give you a head start.'

'Thanks, I appreciate it.'

Kay ended the call and hurried into Sharp's office.

'Obviously, we'll go through the records see if there's anybody who's a match to that DNA,' she said after she'd brought him up to speed on her conversation with the CSI.

'Good,' said Sharp. 'Let me know if we get a match—'

He broke off as Debbie West knocked on the door and entered without waiting for a response.

'You need to see this, guv.'

She handed over a copy of the local newspaper that had been opened to the third page, and jabbed a finger at the article.

Sharp swore.

'What is it?' Said Kay.

Sharp turned the newspaper in his hands so Kay could see the headline. 'Denise Abbott has been talking.'

Kay rose from her chair and took the newspaper from him, running her eyes over the text. She groaned.

Cameron Abbott's widow had single-handedly put the whole investigation at risk. By talking to a reporter, and telling him that the police had been in touch with her to discuss an open case, she had alerted the killer to their progress.

'How much damage has she done, do you think?' said Debbie.

'A lot of this is conjecture,' said Kay. 'At no time did we mention we were investigating a murder, only that there had been another death on the same stretch of railway as her husband.'

'Did you suspect that she might go to the newspapers?' said Sharp.

'Not at all. She seemed to have moved on very quickly after her husband's death. She was seeing someone else, who was at the house when we were there. He didn't introduce himself and remained upstairs.'

'Do you think he was the one that got in touch with the newspaper?'

'Maybe. Look, I'll ask Barnes and Carys to go around to see them both and reiterate that they're not to talk to the press about this investigation again.'

'Do that. I'll get our media officer to call the newspaper's editor and have a word. Hopefully we can salvage this.' Sharp glanced over her shoulder, and Kay followed his gaze.

Her heart sank.

DCI Larch was stalking across the incident room towards them, his face a shade of beetroot.

'Debbie, get back to your desk. You're not needed here,' said Sharp.

Debbie scuttled from the office, relief across her features.

Larch slammed the door and Kay braced herself for the onslaught.

'What the bloody hell have you done, Hunter?' He stabbed his finger at her, spittle on his lips. He snatched the newspaper from her grasp and held it in front of her face, his hands shaking. 'Was this your idea? We have media policies for a reason, Detective Sergeant.'

'Guv, this had nothing to do with Kay,' said Sharp, his voice calm. He reached out and lowered the newspaper, ignoring the DCI's glare. 'Denise Abbott chose to go to the press of her own accord. We can only assume she wanted the attention, but we've tasked Barnes and Miles to go round to her house immediately and explain the nature of our investigation and request she refrain from speaking to anyone else in the media.'

'It's not good enough, Sharp. Wherever Hunter goes, there's trouble. Sort it out, for chrissakes.'

He spun on his heel, flung the door open, and strode out of the incident room.

Kay exhaled loudly. 'Thanks, guv.'

'No problem. Look, I know he's got it in for you but don't let him get under your skin. We're under pressure to solve this one quickly. Larch is dealing with budget cuts and performance targets, and he's made it no secret that we're under scrutiny. Let's get on with it before something else conspires to upset him.'

Kay couldn't help herself. 'Or else heads will roll?'

Sharp's eyes narrowed and he tried to suppress a

smirk. 'You've been hanging around with Barnes again, haven't you? I should—'

He stopped mid-sentence as Carys rushed into the room. 'Guv? I got a call from Lucas – he said you need to check your emails. He's managed to get a match on our victim's dental records.'

'Get the team together, Carys. I'll join you in a second.'

He rushed back to his computer, and Kay hurried to her desk to grab her notebook.

An excited murmur filled the room as the team left their desks and made their way to where Sharp stood with his back to the whiteboard. He didn't wait for them to settle. 'We have a positive identification for our victim.'

The room fell silent.

'Lawrence Whiting. Aged forty-four. Currently unemployed, he'd been renting a flat in Larkfield for the past year.' He passed the full report to Kay. 'You all know what to do. Track down and notify the next of kin. His GP's details are in the report so start there. Interview his family and friends, sort out access to the flat. Somebody might have a spare set of keys, otherwise get the locksmith there as soon as possible.'

CHAPTER EIGHTEEN

Kay frowned as Barnes moved into the inner lane off the bypass and turned onto the motorway.

'I thought you said Lawrence's mother lived in Allington?'

'She used to. When I spoke to the receptionist at his GP's surgery, it turns out his mother has been diagnosed with the early symptoms of dementia. The receptionist gave me the sister's phone number. She and Lawrence arranged to move their mother to a nursing home the other side of Aylesford. The sister, Grace, will meet us there. I've asked Hazel to meet us there, as well.'

Hazel Aldridge was one of the team's family liaison officers, whose role involved providing support to bereaved families while an investigation took place. An invaluable member of the team, Hazel had skills that meant she was best placed to provide the family with regular updates about the investigation, and deal with any questions they might have about the process.

Kay had a lot of admiration for anyone who took on the role, as it could often be very confronting when dealing with others' frustration and grief.

They reached the aged care facility within twenty minutes, the volume of traffic steady between the daily school run and commuter rush. Barnes pulled the car into a space next to Hazel's vehicle, and led the way into the reception area.

Kay was struck by the sense of false cheer created by colourful plants in pots either side of the front door and bright colours that had been applied to the walls of the reception area. The thick carpet muted their footsteps while a faint trace of disinfectant filled the air.

Hazel pushed herself out of one of the comfy-looking armchairs in reception as they entered, and shook hands with them both. 'I've signed in, and they've arranged to let us have the use of the day room while the other residents are having an afternoon tea in the canteen.'

Kay's shoulders relaxed a little. It was typical of Hazel to take charge of the situation, for which she was grateful. She signed the register after Barnes, and the receptionist provided directions to the day room.

'Mrs Whiting and her daughter are already there,' she said. 'The room is all yours for the next forty minutes.'

Kay followed Barnes and Hazel along a carpeted corridor that seemed to use an inordinate amount of beige compared to the cheery reception area. Although it was well lit, a dreariness clung to the walls and a sensation of time slowing down enveloped her.

The corridor ended at a set of double doors, both of which were pegged open and led through to the day room. A selection of armchairs had been scattered around the space in small groups, and Kay was surprised to find the decor to be modern and uplifting compared to the corridor. She wondered if the interior decorating budget only stretched so far, and to the places more likely to be used by visiting families, then chastised herself for her cynicism.

Large patio windows overlooked a paved terrace that led to well-tended gardens lined with a border of fir trees. A television had been fixed to the left-hand wall of the room, while various colourful pictures filled the plasterwork around it.

A woman rose from a two-seater sofa against the right-hand wall, and made her way towards them. Her short brown hair had been cut into a severe bob, the sides of which she tucked behind her ears, revealing two studs in one earlobe. A plain-looking woman, she appeared to have aged prematurely as if her mother's and brother's health had been having a detrimental effect on her own.

'Grace Whiting?'

The woman nodded.

'I'm Detective Sergeant Kay Hunter. I'm sorry for your loss.'

The woman shook her hand, and blinked back tears before dabbing at her cheeks with a scrunched up paper tissue she held in her other hand. 'Thank you, Detective. I've let our mother know, but as you can see, I'm not sure she's understood.'

She gestured to the woman sitting in the armchair next to the sofa with a blanket drawn up over her knees. The woman smiled and gave a little wave before confusion swept across her features and she dropped her hand to her lap.

Kay introduced Barnes and Hazel.

'Hazel will be your family liaison officer while we continue our investigations. She'll be able to answer any questions you might have about our progress and the process. Would you mind if we ask you some questions about your brother?'

'That's fine. Shall we take a seat over here, and I can keep my mother company at the same time?'

She turned and settled into a second armchair, sweeping her grey wool calf-length skirt underneath her before pulling her pale yellow cardigan around her shoulders. She dropped her hands into her lap and began to play with the wedding band on her finger.

Barnes extracted his notebook, and Kay nodded her thanks. With one of them taking notes, she could concentrate on listening to Grace.

'We weren't very close,' she began. 'He had his own health issues to deal with, and when our mum was diagnosed with dementia six months ago, it was left to me to look after her.'

Kay noted the undertone of bitterness in the woman's voice. 'Did he ever visit your mother here?'

'Not to my knowledge. I think he was embarrassed. He struggled to cope with his depression, and had managed to start to turn his life around. I don't think he wanted the responsibility on top of everything else.'

'When was the last time you saw your brother?'

'About four weeks ago. We have to put Mum's house on the market to pay for her accommodation here and so I was starting to clear through her things. I found some bits and pieces of his amongst her stuff in the attic, and suggested he take a look at it to see if he wanted to keep any of it. He called in, but he didn't hang around. He was probably there for all of an hour, no more.'

'Can you think of anyone who would have wanted to harm your brother?'

'No. When Lawrence's depression became too much, he lost touch with a lot of his old friends. It's the same old story with mental illness, isn't it? People don't know how to react to it, or help and so they drift away. The problem is, when Lawrence was feeling low he couldn't help the way he acted. People took it as being rude, but it was simply the case that he couldn't cope being around people – it made him too anxious. So, in answer to your question, I can't think of anybody that would want to harm him, because he wasn't socialising with anybody.'

'How did he seem, the last time you saw him?'

A sad smile crossed the woman's face. 'He looked healthier, as if he was eating properly and getting some exercise for a change. While he'd been out of work, he put a lot of weight on and the antidepressants probably didn't help with that. But when I saw him that day, he seemed more upbeat. He was even talking about applying for a job he'd seen in the paper that week. It was such a change in behaviour for him because when he was ill, he seemed to lose the will to live.'

CHAPTER NINETEEN

Kay followed Gavin across the road towards the three-storey block of flats.

After tracking down and speaking with Whiting's sister, Kay and Barnes had spent some time with her providing their contact numbers and listening while Hazel explained her role and availability, before leaving with a spare set of keys she held for her brother's flat.

She hadn't wanted to accompany them.

'You're welcome to take what you need,' she said. 'I don't think I can face going there at the moment.'

Kay had dropped off Barnes at the police station so he could update the investigation database with his notes, and set off for Larkfield with Gavin in tow, much to Carys's chagrin.

'I can help you search the flat,' she'd said, after pulling Kay to one side while her colleague grabbed his jacket.

'I realise that,' said Kay, 'but I'm taking Gavin. You've had plenty of experience at doing this.'

Crestfallen, Carys had turned away and busied herself making small talk with Barnes about the morning's events.

Now, Kay inserted the first of three keys into a locked door that led into a wide hallway flagged by the first of four flats on the ground floor.

Gavin made sure the doors were shut behind them and the security mechanism had locked before leading the way up two flights of stairs and along the landing. He stopped at the second door on the right and glanced at the aluminium numbers screwed to its surface.

'This is the one.'

They paused to pull protective gloves over their hands, and then entered the flat.

Apart from a slight musty smell, the flat appeared to be clean and tidy. A narrow hallway led to a bedroom off to the right with a bathroom next to it. The kitchen and lounge room area had been recently renovated, and comprised one large living area.

Muted daylight poured through a front window that had Venetian blinds pulled down for privacy. A television sat on a low unit under the window, the remote control to one side of it. Here and there on the walls, a selection of cheap photographic prints had been hung. Kay recognised them from a shop she often passed in the Fremlin Walk shopping centre.

She moved over the threshold and into the kitchen, her eyes taking in the tidy worktops – a bottle of olive oil stood next to the cooker hob, and a selection of condiments were lined up neatly against the tiles that lined the wall. She turned and opened the refrigerator door, and was surprised to see a selection of fresh vegetables and fruit amongst the jars of half-used pasta sauce, mustards, and plastic containers.

'He was certainly looking after himself,' said Gavin.

'His sister told us that he'd recently become more interested in healthy eating. She said he'd put a lot of weight on due to the depression and the drugs he was on.'

Gavin pointed to a set of weights in the corner. 'Out of all of the victims we're investigating, he seems to be the only one that was starting to turn his life around with any success.'

Kay slammed the refrigerator door. 'All the more reason to find out who murdered him. Right, you take the bedroom while I continue in here. Let's see if there's anything that might help us.'

As Gavin passed, she began to pull out the drawers under the worktop. The top drawer was taken up by a selection of cutlery, while the next three contained a mixture of half used packets of batteries, a screwdriver set, pack of cards, and various plastic boxes that upon closer inspection contained a small sewing kit and shoe polishing items.

She turned her attention to the cupboards above the hob, and pushed back the collection of plates, coffee mugs and glassware.

Finding nothing, she turned and then crouched down

to open the cupboard under the sink, and turned off the water supply.

After working her way through the expansive food cupboards, she moved to the living area.

She tutted under her breath at the state of the bookshelves and DVD collection. Plastic cases were balanced on each other in a haphazard way, and a discarded cigarette packet lay scrunched up next to a pile of books.

She began in the top left-hand corner of the bookshelves and began to flick through the pages of the novels one by one, in the hope that a receipt or a note might be discovered.

There was nothing.

She wandered through to the bedroom where Gavin crouched on his hands and knees, his head in the wardrobe.

'Found anything?'

He extracted himself, and shook his head. 'There are some boxes and things at the bottom here, but nothing of interest. Just old photo albums and magazines. Some old clothes – they look like they've been used for gardening or something.' He straightened and gestured around the room. 'Bed was made. Nothing underneath. I'll check the bedside cabinet in a minute.'

'All right, I'm going to see what's in the bathroom.'

After opening the toilet cistern to make sure nothing untoward had been stowed within, Kay moved to the separate bathroom.

A shower rose hung over the bath, the controls for

an electric pump fastened to the wall beneath it, while a plain white unit with a wide bowl on top of it had replaced the original sink unit during the landlord's renovations.

Kay opened each drawer in the vanity unit, sifting through various packets of headache tablets and razor attachments, then slammed the last one shut in frustration.

Despite knowing who their victim was, they were still no closer to finding out why he died, or who had killed him.

'Sarge?'

Gavin appeared at the door, a diary in his hand. 'Found something. The afternoon Whiting was killed, he had an appointment with someone called Simon Ancaster in the afternoon. There's a phone number, too.'

'Right,' said Kay. 'Let's see what Mr Ancaster has to say for himself, shall we?'

CHAPTER TWENTY

A renewed energy filled the incident room when Kay and Gavin returned, the team galvanised now they had a name for their victim and could begin to piece together his background.

The stuffy atmosphere was filled with the aroma of print toner and burnt coffee as the investigating team pored over reports and other documentation, trying to piece together the case.

Kay peeled her jacket off her shoulders. The only problem with the centrally controlled heating system was it was temperamental. Some days, it could be freezing cold upstairs and on others like this, when it was packed to the rafters with a full investigation team, the air was static.

Barnes often complained how cold the interview rooms were by comparison, and Kay had told him hot air rose. His response was to make a remark about all the managers and chiefs on the top floor. Smiling at the memory, Kay placed her jacket on the back of her chair, knowing that within the hour the thermostat could reset to an Arctic blast and they'd all be huddled in their jackets trying to keep warm.

Carys had overcome her dismay at being left out of the search after discovering nothing had been found to advance the investigation, and seemed content to laugh and joke with Gavin while they made a round of tea in preparation for the afternoon briefing.

Kay smiled, typing up her notes into the case database and fielding a couple of urgent emails as she listened to their good-natured banter.

Running a murder investigation was stressful enough, without the team becoming fractious with each other.

She checked her watch. In an hour, the incident room would be emptying for the afternoon.

A thought had occurred to her earlier that day, and it was all she could do to try to concentrate on the investigation. Her conversation with Adam earlier in the week kept going around in her head. He was right, it would be a risk using one of the computers in the incident room to conduct her own research, but she couldn't think of another way.

She leaned back in her chair and cast her eyes around the room at her colleagues. However much she enjoyed working with them, it scared her that one of them could be responsible for putting the blame on her for the missing evidence that had led to the Professional Standards investigation. She had been careful to ensure that she left nothing of a personal nature in her drawer at work. There was nothing in her locker, either. She hated not being able to trust anyone, but first and foremost she had to make sure she found out the truth, and that nothing could be used to compromise her career again.

At least DCI Larch had kept his distance for the remainder of the day. The less interaction she had to deal with, the less she felt she was being constantly judged. Whenever he was around, it was as if he were waiting for her to make a mistake so he could pounce.

Now that she had made up her mind though, impatience threatened common sense. It was so tempting to use the database now to research the old case, but there were too many people around. She wasn't sure she could explain herself if one of them saw what she was doing. Yes, she had told Adam it was natural for her to want to know why she had been set up, and what had happened to the missing evidence, but she still didn't want to have to explain herself to any of her colleagues.

'Penny for your thoughts?'

She jumped at the sound of Barnes's voice over her shoulder. 'Sorry, I didn't hear you.'

'Yeah, you looked like you were deep in thought. What's wrong?'

'It's okay. Nothing. Just trying to get my thoughts together in order to type up my report for today.'

'Did you find out much at Whiting's flat?'

'Nothing at all really. I did get the impression that his sister was right, and he was trying to turn his life around again. The fridge was jam-packed with healthy food, and he had a set of weights in the living room. We didn't find anything to suggest that he knew his killer, or why he was killed though. There were no drugs in the flat. Just some headache pills, so this isn't looking like a drugs deal gone wrong or anything like that.'

'And he wasn't on the rehabilitation programme.' Barnes sat down in his chair with a sigh as Carys and Gavin approached. 'So, it doesn't look like the two we interviewed about the programme are involved then.'

'It's something to do with the antidepressants though,' said Kay. 'It feels right, somehow.'

'But apart from the drink driving course, we haven't found anything to connect Lawrence to the other two,' said Carys.

'And we didn't find any antidepressants at Whiting's flat,' added Gavin. 'He might have been prescribed them once, but he's not now.'

'I've been thinking about that, and it doesn't make sense. Lucas managed to take some blood samples and his report states there's traces of antidepressants in Whiting's system, so where's his supply?'

'Do you think his killer removed them from the flat?' said Carys.

'Maybe. I'm waiting to speak with Lawrence's GP,' said Kay. 'See if we can find out why he was put on antidepressants in the first place, and when his most recent prescription was. There has to be a link there somewhere.'

'When are you going to see him?'

'His receptionist said he only works three days a week. We've missed him this afternoon, so I'm expecting him to call back the day after tomorrow.'

'What about Whiting's work history, or anything like that?'

'He's been out of work for a couple of months. He had a job stacking shelves at a builder's merchants for about six months before that, but according to his sister when Lawrence's depression and anxiety became too much, he couldn't cope. It sounds like his employers tried to do what they could, but in the end they had to let him go. Maybe that gave him the incentive to try to work with his illness to improve his life? It'll be interesting to see what his GP has to say, that's for sure.'

Barnes jabbed his pen at Carys and Gavin. 'It'd be a good idea if you two go and speak to his manager at the builder's merchants tomorrow. Find out what sort of issues his depression caused, and whether something happened there that led to his murder.'

'Will do,' said Carys. 'Are there any friends of his we can speak to as well?'

Kay shook her head. 'According to his sister, a lot of his friends drifted away as his depression worsened. She wasn't able to give us a list of anybody we could talk to, but Gavin's trying to get hold of someone called Simon Ancaster, whose details we found in Whiting's diary. In the meantime, if Lawrence's employer has any other contacts we can speak to, then get a note of those while you're there. We need all the help we can muster at the moment to get a breakthrough.'

She glanced over her shoulder as Sharp emerged from his office. 'All right, let's get the boss up to speed during this briefing, and then hopefully tomorrow we'll have better luck.'

CHAPTER TWENTY-ONE

He shoved his hands into the pockets of the light anorak, and eased his pace to what he hoped was a nonchalant stroll.

The man was several metres in front of him, completely unaware that he was being watched, and that every move he had made for the past month had been carefully observed and recorded.

Now, it was time for all his careful planning to be tested.

He had stayed up late the previous night, checking and rechecking his calculations. Once the sun had dipped over the trees at the back of the garden, he'd drawn the curtains so the neighbour couldn't see through the window and wonder why he was working so late in the garage.

A calmness settled on him as he walked, his target's form weaving between other pedestrians.

He had made the phone call earlier that morning. He had waited until the street outside had quietened, his neighbours disappearing off to work or to regular shopping trips. He knew the man didn't leave his flat much, and that his day-to-day life probably revolved around watching the world go by his window. A phone call mid-morning would be unexpected.

His assumptions had been correct. The man had answered the phone, his voice cautious.

He explained to him that he would like to meet, that it had been too long since he had last been in touch.

The man had seemed wary at first, but had eventually agreed to meet later that day after he had explained why they should talk.

Now, he picked up his pace to keep the man in his sights.

His shoulder bumped against a woman laden with shopping bags, and he apologised in a low voice.

She grumbled under her breath, but hurried past him after making eye contact, and he wondered what she saw there.

Did he look like a killer?

He suspected not. That's what worked to his advantage.

He had been shocked by his appearance in the reflection of the window of the supermarket he'd passed earlier. He acknowledged that his project had become an obsession, but he hadn't accounted for the effect it would have on his body.

He tried to remember when he had last eaten properly. These days, he seemed to sustain himself on a diet of coffee and the occasional drive-through meal. He had lost weight, of that he was sure. He didn't own a set of bathroom scales but he'd had to cinch his belt an extra notch over the past couple of months, and his shirts seemed looser.

The calculations and plans that he'd worked on for weeks tumbled around in his thoughts. When he had first started, he had taken his notes with him. He'd been so afraid that he'd got his calculations wrong. He needn't have worried. His mind was still sharp, and everything had gone to plan.

His confidence had grown with each completed project.

Until the last time.

The old paranoia had returned. He berated himself that his plans had been compromised. He had wanted to remain in control all the time; however, the police were now involved and that changed matters.

The man in front of him reached the pedestrian crossing, and he held back, not wanting to be seen. Not yet. He couldn't reveal himself until the right moment. He turned, as if to read an advert displayed on the nearby bus shelter, and waited until he heard the familiar *zap* of the crossing lights.

He let the man cross ahead of him, and then followed him along the busy street. As they passed the post office, the man turned his attention to the bustling crowds on Wheeler Street, then decided to continue onwards.

He smiled. The man was predictable.

Before the phone call this morning, he had followed the man over the past few weeks. He had never been seen; he had been too careful. He couldn't afford for the man to notice him, not yet, otherwise the whole plan could fall apart.

He hadn't lied to him when he spoke to him this morning. It had been a long time since he had spoken with any of them. After everything that had happened, they had all drifted away. His fists clenched in his pockets.

After a few paces, his quarry turned right and continued walking along a narrow pedestrianised lane that spat them out next to the little theatre. The man checked the road left and right, and then jogged across and through the doors of a pub.

Satisfied his target was at their designated meeting place, he waited for a moment and leaned against the wall of the theatre. He glanced up at the sky. The county town hadn't yet shrugged off the bitter chill of winter, and heavy clouds churned the sky grey. It was time to get inside, before it started to rain.

He pushed through the narrow double doors into the pub, and made his way over to the bar. He knew where the man sat, but he averted his gaze. He wanted to control the situation, and make the man come to him.

It was important.

'What will you have?'

'A half of bitter.'

He reached into his pocket for some loose change, and then heard a chair being pushed back across the parquet flooring.

He smiled.

This was going to be even easier than he thought.

CHAPTER TWENTY-TWO

Kay checked over her shoulder at the sound of voices, then relaxed as she realised the cleaners were working their way from room to room.

They wouldn't touch anything in the incident room; each person was responsible for putting their wastepaper basket outside the door ready to be emptied, and anything of a confidential nature that wasn't required for the case file would go into a confidential waste bin located outside Sharp's office.

She reached out for the mug of coffee next to her, then recoiled as she realised the china was stone cold.

She pushed the coffee away and logged into the HOLMES2 database, before waiting as the server caught up with her fast keystrokes. Her eyes fell to the clock displayed in the bottom right-hand corner of the screen. She didn't want to be late; it was rare that she and Adam spent time together during the week, but it had been weeks since she'd got the office to herself, and she couldn't access the database at home.

And she couldn't take the risk during the day, not with so many people around.

She bit her lip. She didn't doubt that she could trust the others on the team, but after the fallout following the Professional Standards investigation into missing evidence that had put a stop to her promotion to detective inspector, and the unspoken inferences that it was she who had lost that evidence on purpose, she wasn't prepared to risk anyone else's career.

Especially when she wasn't sure who she could trust.

Not yet.

She'd had her innocence proven, but the rumours remained, and she was met with an air of distrust among many of her colleagues.

Eventually, the computer caught up with her keystrokes and opened up the file for the case she had been involved with.

Jozef "Joe" Demiri was one of the county's most unsavoury characters. Kent Police had been monitoring his activities over the past couple of years, but to date had been unsuccessful in collating enough information to charge him.

Originally from Albania, he ran a network of lackeys and go-to men who carried out his work, ensuring that none of their criminal activities could be used against him. Kay and her colleagues, including DCI Larch, were convinced that Demiri was involved in both drugs and human trafficking but the people he employed were too terrified to speak, such was his reputation for violence against those that tried to cross him.

The south coast of Kent was beginning to get a reputation for people smuggling due to the lack of resources available to patrol the waters of the English Channel. The flat country and beaches around the old Cinque Ports provided ample opportunity for boats to enter the waters with their precious cargo.

It had been pure chance that led to the breakthrough they sought. A uniform patrol had pulled over a van belonging to one of Demiri's men and during a search of the vehicle, a 9mm pistol had been discovered wrapped in an old sweatshirt and stuffed under the passenger seat.

The driver had been arrested, and Kay had been tasked with leading the investigation. It was meant to be the one that would lead to her promotion to detective inspector.

The suspect had refused to talk, but three sets of fingerprints had been taken from the weapon. One set belonged to their suspect, while the other two remained unknown, and Kay was determined to link the gun to Demiri.

It should have been the breakthrough they needed, but they couldn't get to him. At the time the driver was arrested, Demiri was out of the country. Enquiries to his offices at the software company he owned in Ashford resulted in Kay and her colleagues being told he was attending meetings on the Continent and wouldn't fly back for a week.

Kay had settled in for an impatient wait, determined to arrest Demiri upon his return.

And then the gun had disappeared from the evidence locker and her world had disintegrated.

Now, she worked her way through the different modules of the database, her eyes scanning the numerous notes and records she and her colleagues had entered into the system.

Every single phone conversation, interview, evidence record and other lines of enquiry were logged by the team working the case. An exhibits officer had been tasked with logging the various items they had seized over the course of the investigation, including mobile phones, keys to properties that had been searched, and the gun.

Kay's finger froze above her mouse and then she frowned and flicked back two screens to make sure she wasn't mistaken.

She wasn't.

She swore under her breath.

The record describing the gun that had been lodged as evidence was gone.

She scrolled the mouse cursor up and down the page, but it was no good. Someone had deleted the record.

Panic threatened to overwhelm her, and she wiped away the prickle of sweat at her hairline.

There had to be an explanation.

She wracked her memory. She recalled there was a way to look up the history of the online file; a way to find out who entered each update, but she wasn't sure she'd still have administration rights – the secondary login that was needed to review those records, not after her return to active duty.

'Only one way to find out,' she murmured.

She wiggled the mouse as the screen started to darken, and the display brightened immediately. She hovered the cursor over a different menu option, clicked the mouse, and mentally crossed her fingers.

A pop-up message appeared in the middle of the screen.

Password accepted. Please wait.

Kay exhaled.

She leaned forward, counting off the seconds in her head while she waited for the information to download.

And then, after a few seconds, a single name flashed on the screen.

Kay sat back in her chair, and blinked.

'No way,' she breathed.

CHAPTER TWENTY-THREE

Kay walked through the door of her house, and into a hallway filled with the aroma of a roast dinner.

Her stomach rumbled before she'd even slipped the chain over the lock and secured the dead bolt.

'Smells divine,' she said as she entered the kitchen, willing her voice to sound upbeat.

Adam grinned, a joint of beef in a roasting dish between his oven mitt-covered hands. 'You say that about everything you're going to eat.'

'I'm hungry.'

'I guessed that. Go and get out of your work clothes. I've got this under control.'

She swung her bag off her shoulder and left the room as he opened the oven door, the sweet tang of roasting potatoes wafting after her.

She pushed the thought of the missing evidence record to the back of her mind. She couldn't afford to dwell on it; Adam would worry and she still had a murder to solve.

Her mind turned to the death of the man on the railway, and she pulled out her notebook to set herself some reminders for the next day. She liked the challenge, and the more she worked with Sharp, the more he seemed to trust her judgement. She realised it was the confidence boost she needed right now, and the sense that her life was returning to an even keel made her more determined to renew her ambition to become detective inspector.

She quickly undressed, threw her work clothes into the laundry basket, and tugged on a sweatshirt and jeans. Padding back along the landing in bare feet, she paused at the door to the home office.

She stood in the doorway, briefly contemplated whether to switch on the computer and work for half an hour prior to Adam dishing up, and then discounted the idea. She needed time to regroup, to organise her thoughts before she attempted to continue her investigation. She was conscious of the fact that otherwise, she could end up going round in circles.

She needed a breakthrough, and it wasn't going to be found on her home computer.

Instead, she pulled the door closed and made her way downstairs.

'Anything I can do to help?' she said, eyeing up the fresh vegetables Adam had laid out on the chopping board.

'All under control. You could feed Holly, if you like.'

At the sound of her name, the large dog roused herself from her bed and wandered over to her bowl, her tongue hanging out and a smile in her eyes. Her tail bashed the side of the workbench as she waited.

Kay scooped two portions of food into Holly's bowl and set it on the floor next to the back door.

The Great Dane ambled over, sniffed the food once, then tucked in.

'Mmmm. Dog food again.'

'She's happy. Don't tease.' Kay put the plastic scoop back in the bag of dog food and sealed the top, then washed her hands and glanced over her shoulder. 'What've you been up to today?'

Adam joined her at the sink and wrapped his arms around her, his chin on her shoulder as he stared out the kitchen window. The moon had risen over the line of trees beyond the back fence, and now the sky began to speckle with the closest of the evening's stars.

He pointed to the bottom of the garden. 'You have a brand new lock on the garden shed, I've changed the blades on the lawnmower, and I reorganised your CD collection by colour of album cover.'

She spun to face him. 'You did not.'

His mouth quirked. 'Gotcha.'

'Bastard.'

He grinned, and kissed her. 'Yes, but you love me.'

'Just as well.' She picked up the tea towel and swatted him with it.

He laughed and crossed the room to the oven before pulling the glass dish out, its contents crackling and spitting. He swung round and placed it on the chopping board, and then took the carving knife Kay handed over.

The dog paced the floor impatiently, and Kay opened the back door to let her outside.

A breeze lifted her fringe from her forehead and she took a deep breath, savouring the freshness as she stood on the back doorstep. She crossed her arms over her chest and tried to relax. Despite everything, she still had Adam, a roof over her head, and a job she loved.

She stepped aside to let Holly back in, and locked the door.

'Good timing,' said Adam. 'Dinner's served.'

After the plates were stacked in the dishwasher, Kay followed Adam through to the living room, Holly padding after them.

The dog curled up on the carpet in front of the bookshelves against the far wall, and they collapsed onto the sofa.

Kay sighed and patted her stomach. 'I'm stuffed.'

Adam topped up his wineglass with the bottle he'd brought through from the kitchen, and held it up to her.

'Only a bit, thanks.'

'Are you on call tonight?'

'No, but Sharp wants us in early. I don't want a foggy brain in the morning.'

They settled back into the cushions, and Adam scrolled through the channels on the television until he found a music quiz show they both enjoyed.

Soon, they were yelling their answers at the screen and laughing at each other's attempts to outwit the other.

Two hours later, Kay had called it a night.

Except she couldn't sleep.

Adam's soft breathing tickled her ear; he'd fallen asleep with his arm around her and she tried not to fidget in case she woke him up, otherwise she'd be tempted to switch on her bedside lamp and read for a while.

The house creaked as it began to cool down; the central heating had gone off three hours ago, and wouldn't start up again until the early hours of the morning.

Below the bedroom, Holly shuffled on her bed in the kitchen; Kay could hear her through the baby monitor and held her breath in case she needed to wake Adam up because the puppies were on their way. She exhaled as the dog grew silent before soft snores emanated through the monitor, and she smiled.

A car passed by outside, the headlights shining on the ceiling between the cracks in the curtain. It slowed as it passed the house, and Kay frowned, wondering who it could be so late at night. Eventually, it picked up speed as it navigated the bend in the road to the left of the house, its engine fading into the distance.

Kay closed her eyes, and tried to relax.

She was jerked awake by her mobile phone ringing on the bedside table next to her.

She peered through bleary eyes at the number displayed and groaned.

Adam removed his arm from her shoulder. 'Trouble?'

'Sharp.' She took a deep breath before she answered. 'Guv?'

She listened to Sharp's voice, his tone clipped and on edge, then murmured her understanding and finished the call.

Adam's brow creased. 'What's wrong?' he said, as she slipped from beneath the warmth of the bedcovers and began to dress.

'I've got to go. There's been another one.'

CHAPTER TWENTY-FOUR

Kay took one look at Barnes's ashen face, and was glad that when she had attended the scene the previous evening, Sharp had delegated her to interview the train driver with Dave Walker.

'If I'd known how bad that was going to be,' he said, 'I'd have skipped dinner last night.'

Kay rubbed at bleary eyes and tried to push the memory of the last victim from her mind, and returned to the computer to read the notes that had been updated earlier that morning. 'No witnesses this time. The train driver stated he saw nothing to indicate that there was anybody else in the vicinity, either. The first time he saw the body on the tracks, it was because his headlights picked him out. He didn't have time to stop.'

Barnes stared into his coffee, but said nothing.

'Has there been anything to indicate this is another murder, rather than a suicide?' asked Sharp.

'There wasn't much left to work with, guv,' said

Kay. 'I think our killer learned from last time. Whatever he used to keep his victim on those tracks, he didn't tie them down. There's no evidence of rope or plastic ties being used.'

'Drugs?'

'If he used a date rape drug, it's going to be damn hard for Lucas to find that in the body parts he has to work with.'

'So, maybe it is a suicide.'

'I'm not convinced. Not so soon after the last one.'

The phone next to Carys's elbow rang, and Sharp nodded to her to answer it.

'We'll have to run two lines of enquiry into the suicide angle and the murder angle until one of them gets ruled out, then,' he said. 'And that's not going to be easy, given that we don't know who this guy is either.'

'What if he hasn't stopped?' said Barnes. 'What if he's only just getting started?'

'And why start now? Why has he only started killing in the last seven months? What's triggered it?' said Gavin.

Sharp took one of the marker pens and added their questions to the whiteboard. 'Whoever this is, he knows the network well. He's too familiar with the routes in and out of the crime scenes.'

'What about trainspotters?' said Gavin.

'It's worth bearing in mind, but usually they hang around train stations. They're more interested in the locomotives than the routes.'

'Forget suicide. It's murder,' said Carys. She put

down the phone and turned in her chair to face the team. 'That was Harriet on the phone. Her CSI team have just confirmed that although no traces of rope or anything like that were found on the victim, a substance found on the back of his ankles has tested positive as a strong adhesive. The sort you use instead of banging in nails to a wall.'

'Jesus,' said Barnes, breaking the shocked silence. 'He's a monster.'

Sharp paced the carpet in front of the whiteboard. 'Has Harriet confirmed whether any other fingerprints were found on the clothing belonging to the victim?'

Carys shook her head. 'He must have been wearing gloves. Whoever he is, he's well-prepared.'

'Not only does he know how to access areas of track without being seen, he's leaving no evidence behind now,' said Kay. 'He's learning from his mistakes. We were lucky that when Lawrence Whiting was killed, he moved so that the train severed his leg above the ankle and we had the rope as evidence. If he'd remained unconscious and hadn't moved, the wheels of the train would've destroyed the evidence, as our killer originally planned.'

'The footprints Harriet's team found next to the railway tracks,' said Kay, spinning from side to side on her chair while she stared at the whiteboard. 'We all assumed that they were left by our suspect as he left the scene before the train arrived. What if he didn't leave? What if he stayed?'

'To watch, you mean?' Barnes wrinkled his nose. 'That's sick.'

'True. But so is tying a helpless man to a railway line.'

'Doesn't make sense,' said Barnes. 'Why wait so long between kills if it is the same person? He's left it something like a month between the first and second, two months between the second and third, and another two months before Whiting was killed.'

'It could be because if he did it too often, it would raise suspicion.'

'What the hell is his motive?' said Sharp.

'It's not frenzied; it's not like he has an insatiable lust for killing,' said Kay. 'Everything he's done to date has been meticulously planned – even the locations are known suicide spots, and until recently no one else has been around to verify it's murder. If Elsa Flanagan hadn't been walking her dog the other night, we'd be none the wiser.'

'So, he's less likely to make a mistake,' said Barnes. 'Which doesn't help us.'

Kay pointed at the map pinned to the wall. 'And, given the length of track and different routes that cover this area, we've got no idea where he might go next. According to Dave Walker, they've got CCTV cameras at all the stations and some of the bridges that have been used as jumping spots – the rest of the network isn't monitored.'

'What sort of person would do this?' said Carys. 'It's horrific.'

'Someone who wants revenge.' Kay threw down her pen. 'But, for what? And, why the second one so fast?'

'Maybe because the last one went wrong – the victim was able to shout for help,' said Carys. 'And he's probably guessed that someone heard him – if he was still in the area, he might've seen the first responders arrive.'

'Sort of like an arsonist, you mean?' said Barnes.

Carys nodded. 'Exactly.'

'That doesn't make sense,' said Gavin. 'If he knows that we know, surely he'd wait – bide his time as it were, and go into hiding.'

Kay reeled back as if she'd been slapped. 'Shit, that's it,' she said, and looked around at her colleagues.

'He's got a list. Whatever his motive for killing them is, he knows we're on to him, so he's changed his pattern. He wants to make sure he kills them all.'

CHAPTER TWENTY-FIVE

He opened sleep-encrusted eyes and squinted at the bright sunlight that escaped through a chink in the blinds.

Dust motes spun in the air as he stared up at the ceiling and tried to fight down the exhaustion that threatened to engulf him. He twisted his neck and glanced at the alarm clock on the bedside table.

Ten o'clock.

He pushed himself up into an upright position, reached out for the bottle of pills next to the reading lamp, and swallowed two with the aid of the contents of the glass of water he'd left out the night before.

He could hear his neighbour outside, whistling as she hung out her washing. The overly cheerful tune further darkened his mood. He threw back the duvet cover and stomped towards the bathroom.

As he stood under the shower's hot jets of water, his mind turned to the project schedule.

Last night had gone well. This time, he'd carried out a proper risk assessment. There had been no chance of him being discovered, nor his victim, before the train had had a chance to take his life.

It had been perfect. The man had only started to come to his senses within moments of the train's approach.

He reached out for the soap and lathered his body, as he recalled the confusion in the man's eyes when he'd tried to lift his head only to find that he couldn't. He may have been groggy, but he was conscious enough to scream as the train had borne down upon him.

He dried himself, dressed and made his way downstairs to the front room. He peered through the net curtains, but the street was silent. Everyone else had left for work or, like his neighbour, were busy doing household chores.

It was different for him. He was a man of leisure, with no need to work.

Those days were over.

He padded back through the hallway and out the back door, slipped a key from his pocket and wandered round the corner to the elongated garage to the side of the house.

He'd extended the structure to create a workshop for himself several years ago. When he worked, he'd taken up wood turning and had spent hours carving lumps of aged trees into gifts for his friends and work colleagues.

All that had changed.

He glanced over his shoulder at the garden, then

squinted at the azure sky, before making a mental note to mow the lawn before returning to the house.

It wouldn't do to let the place go to wrack and ruin, even if his mind felt like it was disintegrating.

Besides, it would keep him out of the house for a bit longer.

He turned back and inserted the key into the lock and twisted it, the door opening easily on well-greased hinges.

He shut the door and locked it behind him, his hand automatically finding the pull cord for the lights to his right.

Four fluorescent tubes flickered to life amongst the eaves of the garage, illuminating the cobwebs up amongst the roof trusses. He'd insisted on installing a pitched roof after seeing the damage a winter storm had made to his neighbour's flat-roofed garage when the rain had accumulated so much in a short space of time, the entire structure had collapsed onto the contents of the building.

He ran his hand along the edge of the plywood platform that took up the entire back half of his garage.

He couldn't afford for such destruction to occur.

Not yet.

When all this was over, then it would be dismantled.

By others, maybe. Not him.

He lowered himself to the concrete floor and crawled towards the centre of the plywood circle, standing up when he reached the large gap in the middle, and cast his eyes over the landscape before him.

Despite the issues caused by the witness to Whiting's murder, he couldn't help himself. Yesterday, he had driven over to the specialist shop at Canterbury and purchased a new locomotive. The scale model was perfect in every way. He'd seen it in a magazine two months ago and hadn't been able to justify the expense to himself until now. The livery was an exact match to the railway company's rolling stock and as he had carefully unwrapped it upon reaching home, he had salivated as he'd cast away the packaging to reveal his new acquisition.

He had retested his calculations using the new locomotive, not because he doubted his abilities but because it seemed right to use the correct train this time. Maybe it would give him a little extra luck, to make up for the other night.

It wasn't entirely perfect – he'd had to make do with what materials he could buy from the specialist shop in Canterbury, and then make the rest himself.

He didn't mind; he found the creative process a way to relax – a way to still his busy mind, and he often found his best solutions evolved when he was concentrating on making the props that helped to bring each project to life.

His gaze fell on the paperwork strewn across one end of the inner oval. He reached out and gathered up his notes, folding them carefully before placing them on the workbench next to him. He would burn them in the brazier outside later, after he heard his neighbour leave for the supermarket. He couldn't afford for her to notice the smoke, otherwise she'd use it as an excuse to come around and berate him for making her washing stink.

He turned his attention to the array of equipment in front of him. A raised panel contained a series of switches and dials.

His fingers automatically found the power button, which he depressed with a light touch. A whirring sound began from behind where he stood, and a tingle of excitement shot down his spine.

His mouth dry, he heard the sound draw closer as his eyes took in the miniature fields, cattle, and tiny houses.

Another few seconds, and the model train appeared in the corner of his vision. As it rounded the bend, its speed increased and it began to tear down the track towards the tiny figurine that was lying across the steel rails.

He held his breath and leaned closer, his hips brushing against the plywood worktop. The train passed him, and in his mind, he imagined the frantic actions of the driver as he sounded his horn at the vision of the man lying across the rails. At the precise moment, his thumb tweaked the power slightly so that the train began to lose speed.

It was too late.

The model train crashed into the tiny figurine and sent it flying across the fake plastic grass next to the track.

He exhaled as the train disappeared around the next corner and reached out for the figurine with a shaking hand.

He held it up, scrutinising the features where the train's wheels had scratched and torn away at the once smooth moulded surface.

He dropped it to the worktop, picked up a well-thumbed copy of the London to Maidstone timetable and his notebook, and proceeded to work out the calculations for his next project.

CHAPTER TWENTY-SIX

'We need to focus on the location.' Sharp strode over to the map of the area pinned to the wall and pointed at the railway line that started at Maidstone East and stretched across the county and beyond to London Victoria. 'Both Lawrence Whiting and Nathan Cox were killed on this line here. Stephen Taylor wasn't – his body was found on the Strood line. Cameron Abbott was also killed on the Maidstone East to London line. We need to change the parameters of our search. Just because Stephen Taylor and Cameron Abbott attended the same rehabilitation programme, it doesn't mean that their deaths are linked.'

'You mean Stephen Taylor wasn't murdered?'

'Could be. We've assumed so far that he and Cameron were murdered, because they both appear on the attendee list for that programme. But the site of his death doesn't match the others at all. We need to consider the fact that there is another connection. One that eliminates Stephen Taylor but links Nathan Cox, Cameron Abbott, and Lawrence Whiting.'

'And our latest victim. Whoever he is.'

'Nothing we can identify him with?'

Barnes shook his head. 'Same as the last one. No wallet, no wedding ring, nothing. Whoever our killer is, he's smart.'

'Any idea from Lucas when he'll do the post mortem?'

'A couple of days. There's a bit of a backlog. He's emailed us some photographs though. I'll get one of the administrators to clean up a photo so we can use it for identification purposes when we're talking to people.'

'Sounds good,' said Sharp. 'Take a copy over to the two guys who run that rehabilitation programme and see if he's one of theirs, so we can rule out that line of enquiry.'

'Will do.'

'Guv, if our killer is so familiar with the footpath and crossings on this stretch of railway, then perhaps we need to look at whether he has worked on the railways at some time, or has another connection with them?' said Carys.

'You're right. The problem is, we're also going to have to widen the investigation to include ramblers' associations, residents whose houses are near to the railway line. I'd like us to be in a position to narrow down that search before we do so. We simply don't have the manpower.'

Sharp ran a hand over his close-cropped hair and

paced the carpet in front of them. 'Why is he killing now? I think you've got a point, Hunter, that he has a list, but what triggered the killings? Notwithstanding the fact we now think Stephen Taylor's death was suicide, we still have four deaths closely linked within a four-month timeframe. What was he waiting for? Or what happened to make him start killing?'

'Are you sure our killer is a man?' said Gavin.

'It's a good question,' said Sharp. 'However, you've got to take into account whoever the killer is, he or she has had to move a body from a car to a railway line. That's involved some steep terrain, and given that we're presuming he's drugging his victims first, those bodies are going to be heavy. In the circumstances, I don't think we're looking for a woman.'

'It's a particularly savage way of killing someone, too,' said Carys. 'To me, it's the sort of thing a man would do, not a woman.'

'I'm inclined to agree. Our killer is being particularly careful to ensure his victims are killed by a train running over them, and not by the electrical current running through the third rail. Both Lawrence Whiting's and our latest victim's bodies have been positioned against the inside rail. Whoever our killer is, he's making a point. He's not giving his victims an opportunity to kill themselves; he's maintaining control throughout. Whoever he is, he's exerting a lot of self-discipline.'

'Have we heard from Simon Ancaster yet?'

'Got a phone call from him earlier, guv,' said

Barnes. 'He was at work this morning, but I've made arrangements for us to speak to him after we're done here. I got the impression he was genuinely shocked about Whiting's death, so he might not be our killer.'

'There's something else,' said Kay. 'All the other deaths have occurred during the late afternoon and early evening commuter rush. Last night's death was caused by an empty train returning to the depot. It wasn't carrying any passengers. None of the other deaths happened that late before.'

'Why do you think the pattern has changed?'

'First, less chance of him being seen, obviously. Second, that empty train would have been travelling at a considerable speed. Okay, the driver wasn't breaking any speed limits, but nor did he have to worry about slowing down to stop at stations.'

'So he wouldn't have been able to stop even if he wanted to.'

Sharp's lips thinned. 'He's learning from his mistakes. Whoever he is, and despite what we think about him increasing his frequency, he must have been planning this for months. He knows the train lines back to front, he knows the timetables, and he knows exactly when the last trains are run back to the depot.'

'Perhaps it's time we asked Dave Walker and his team to start questioning employees of the railway company. Ask for a list of anyone who's lost their job prior to that first suspected killing seven months ago,' said Kay. She held up her hand to stop him interrupting. 'I know, it will take time. But we can't rule it out.'

'But what's the motive?'

'Maybe somebody got made redundant and holds a grudge against them. Maybe our killer blames the railway company for something.'

'Maybe our killer is a passenger who got pissed off with the number of rail strikes on this line,' Barnes grumbled.

CHAPTER TWENTY-SEVEN

Kay stepped to one side and let Barnes lead the way through the gap in the dilapidated garden wall.

To her left, an overflowing wheelie bin threatened to topple over, the distinct smell of discarded pizza boxes escaping from its contents. She side-stepped a pile of old newspapers that had been bound together and tossed onto the path near the bin, and wrinkled her nose at the overgrown garden.

She turned her attention to the house. It had borne the brunt of being tenanted over the years; paint flaked from the plain front door, and the whole building carried an air of neglect.

Barnes rang the doorbell, and turned to face her. 'Nice place.'

Kay rolled her eyes at him before the door opened.

'Simon Ancaster?'

'Yes?'

Kay held up her warrant card, and introduced herself and Barnes.

'We wondered if we could talk to you about Lawrence Whiting.'

'Of course. I'm sorry, it still hasn't really sunk in that he's gone.'

He led them through to a cluttered living room, and began to gather up magazines, takeaway cartons and an ashtray. He had the decency to look embarrassed.

'I don't often get visitors.'

He seemed unsure what to do with the items now in his hands. In the end, he strode over to a low table and dropped everything onto it. He turned back to them. 'Please, have a seat.'

Kay took one look at the stained sofa, raised her eyebrow at Barnes, and resigned herself to doing an extra load of laundry that evening. She lowered herself onto the cushions, and waited while Ancaster settled in an armchair beside the television.

'Simon, I understand that you knew Lawrence Whiting?'

'That's right.'

'Were you close?'

'We got on like a house on fire. We met at grammar school and used to hang around together when we both got motorbikes. Only small ones, mind, but it used to impress the girls.' His mouth quirked at the memory. 'He was a really good laugh. I didn't see him that often, especially when he started suffering from depression, but I tried to leave a message on his phone once a month

– you know, to let him know I was worried about him. He came over the other week at last, and I was surprised to see him looking so well after all he's been through.'

Kay nodded at the correlation with Ancaster's story matching the entry in Whiting's diary.

'What was his state of mind when you saw him?'

'He seemed fine. Nothing to indicate that he was contemplating suicide. Still can't believe it.'

'Can you describe your movements on the day Lawrence died?'

His eyebrows shot up. 'Why do you want to know?'

'Please answer the question.'

'I went to work as usual. Lawrence knocked on the door about an hour after I got home – we chatted over a coffee and I was going to suggest we walk down to the pub to have a drink when his phone rang. I made myself scarce – it was pretty obvious it was a private call, but when I came back to the kitchen, he had his coat on and said he had to leave. I was surprised, because I thought he was still struggling with the social side of things. I was happy to see that he was making some progress, but a bit pissed off at him going so soon after he'd arrived, especially as we hadn't seen each other for weeks, so I asked him who he was meeting. He wouldn't say, only that it was someone he used to know. He was really cagey about it when I questioned him. He told me to leave it alone, and that the person had asked to meet him in confidence.'

'Was he normally so secretive about who he was

meeting? You said earlier that you got on like a house on fire.'

'I did think it a bit odd, but look – it wasn't any of my business, so I didn't push it. I thought maybe it was to do with his treatment or something.'

'What do you do for a living?'

'I teach at the local primary school.'

'What time did you get home from work?'

'About three-fifteen. There was a burst water main in the boys' toilets, so the headmaster took the decision to close the school for the day.' He smiled. 'I remember thinking at the time that at least it'd give me a chance to get home and changed out of my work clothes before Lawrence arrived.'

'And what time did Lawrence leave?'

'He was gone by five o'clock. I remember because I looked at the clock on the oven. It was all a bit strange, to be honest.'

'In what way?'

'Well, he's never been the sort of person to go out of his way to socialise, and if he went to the pub it was usually because I dragged him there – and that'd be later in the day.'

'And you had no contact with him after he left the house?'

He shook his head.

'All right,' said Kay. 'We appreciate your time, thank you.' She handed over one of her business cards. 'Please, if you think of anything else, give me a call.'

As they were walking back to the car, her mind

replayed the conversation. Barnes walked beside her in silence, knowing better than to interrupt her thoughts. Finally, she stopped and placed a hand on his arm.

'If Lawrence left the house at five o'clock, and Elsa Flanagan didn't see him on the tracks until quarter to seven, where did he go?'

'And where's his mobile phone?'

'Harriet and her team didn't find anything at the scene – that's why it took so long for him to be identified.'

'So, the killer enticed him out of the house and they arranged to meet somewhere. Wherever that was, Whiting's killer overpowered him and tied him to the railway tracks, and then took all his belongings?'

'Or, did he meet someone else, and then the killer followed him from there?' Kay shook her head and began walking once more. 'Too many questions, Ian. We've still got a long way to go with this one.'

'Twenty-eight.'

CHAPTER TWENTY-EIGHT

Kay always experienced a heightened sense of awareness when talking to the parents of a murder victim.

Although their son had died four months ago and someone else had broken the news, at the time Nathan Cox's parents were under the impression he had killed himself. She couldn't imagine what it must be like for them to discover that, in all likelihood, he had been murdered.

'What's the background about the parents?'

Carys cast her eyes over the printout in her hand, which she had extracted from the HOLMES2 database. 'Derek Cox is a retired long-distance truck driver. His wife, Rose, used to work as a claims officer for one of the insurance companies in town; she hasn't returned to work since her son died. According to the coroner's inquest report into Nathan's death, he had been living with them for three months prior to his death.'

'How old was he when he died?'

'Twenty-eight.'

'Married, or a girlfriend?'

'No one noted here. No one came forward when his death was announced in the paper, either.'

'What about siblings?'

'No, he was an only child.'

'Christ.' Kay sighed. 'Okay, let's get on with this.'

Nathan's father opened the door, shook hands with them both and showed them through to the kitchen.

A large space, the walls had been painted a cheery bright yellow while the worktops held a high sheen. Kay noted the lemony scent of a popular household cleaner, and realised the couple had made the effort especially for her and Carys. Her heart went out to them, and she hoped that they had a solid network of friends to support them in their grief.

Both Derek and his wife fussed over them for a moment, and so it was several minutes before tea orders had been taken, the kettle boiled and the four of them settled around a circular pine table.

'Thank you for taking the time to see us,' said Kay. 'I understand this must be difficult for you and I understand my colleague here has already phoned you to let you have an update about our investigation and how it may affect the original coroner's inquest into Nathan's death.'

Derek reached across for his wife's hand and wrapped his fingers around hers. 'To be honest, we were relieved. For the past four months I've been trying to understand why our son would take his own life. Obviously, we're upset that another man has lost his life, but if it means that the police are now investigating Nathan's death once more, then at least we might get some answers.'

'What was your relationship like with Nathan?'

'Oh, we had our ups and downs – like any family, I suppose. Everyone expects us to say that because he was depressed, he was difficult to live with. It couldn't be more different. He was prescribed some new medication about six weeks before he was killed by that train. Of course, it took about four weeks before the drug started to work, but he had turned a corner and we'd really noticed a difference in his demeanour. He started talking about finding work again, perhaps as a bus driver because they were advertising for casual staff at the time.'

'I know this is probably painful to revisit, but can you take me back to the events of that day?'

Rose leaned forward and wrapped her fingers around her tea mug, despite the fact the hot surface must have been burning her skin.

'Derek was on an overnight trip to Poland and wasn't due back until that night. I'd left for work as usual. Thank goodness we had said goodbye properly,' she said, and used the heel of her hand to wipe her eyes. 'As I was leaving, Nathan told me that he was planning to walk to the newsagents to pick up a copy of that week's newspaper – they always have the jobs in there on a Friday, and he wanted to see if there were some different ones to those he'd found by searching online. Sometimes I have to work late, especially if we've got a court case coming up. There's always so much to do, organising all the paperwork and making sure experts have everything they need before the date.'

Kay waited patiently, letting the woman tell her story at her own pace.

'I suppose it was about five forty-five in the afternoon. I'd heard from our receptionist that the trains had been delayed. Her fiancé works in the city and had phoned her to tell her he was going to be late home. I didn't think anything of it. There were four of us working in the office at the time, and I remember standing at the photocopier when one of them came over to me and told me that the police were in reception and wanted to see me. They took me into the little meeting room in a corner of the office, and told me Nathan had lain down across the tracks. The train driver didn't see him in time—'

She broke off as tears rolled down her cheeks.

Kay reached into her bag to pull out a packet of paper tissues, and passed them across the kitchen table to her. 'I'm sorry, Mrs Cox. I have to ask these questions.'

'I know.' Rose sniffed, wiped at her eyes, and then held the bunched-up tissue in her fist. 'I kept wondering whether I missed something. Like I said, we had no idea he was still struggling to cope.'

Derek placed his hand on his wife's arm before turning to Kay. 'I wondered at the time whether he had stopped taking the antidepressants for some reason. I know that doesn't make sense, but I thought that he reckoned he could manage without them.'

'Do you know if he *had* stopped taking them?'

'I'm not sure,' said Derek. 'He used to take them when he had breakfast in the morning and often we were already out of the house by then. They were really strong. He only had to take them once a day.'

'That's the thing,' said Rose. 'Nathan never gave us any indication that his depression was so bad that he'd considered suicide. His medication was working, and he was starting to get out and socialise with some of his old friends again.'

'Do you have a note of those friends?' said Kay. 'We'd like to talk to them as well, to see if maybe they can help us with our enquiries.'

'Of course. Hang on.'

Kay waited while Rose stood up and moved across to a set of drawers under the microwave. She pulled each of them out and rummaged through the contents, until she found what she was looking for.

'Here you go. This was Nathan's mobile phone. I couldn't bear to throw it out for some reason. You'll need this charger. I think all his contacts are still saved in there.'

Kay took the mobile charger and phone from her. 'That's great, thank you very much. I'll make sure this is returned to you as soon as possible.'

Rose nodded, and sat back down before dabbing at her eyes once more. 'The sad thing is, some days I'm so angry that he left us that way, and on others I can't remember what his face looked like.'

CHAPTER TWENTY-NINE

Kay found that she could only sing along to the radio in the car if no one else was in the vehicle with her, which was why she was belting out the chorus to an old Eighties hit by The Cult when she turned into her street.

The words dried up as she drew level with her house, her elderly neighbour glaring at her in the beam from the car headlights. She turned down the volume and nodded to the man before swinging the car in past the gate posts and onto the driveway. Turning off the ignition, she frowned.

Holly was barking from inside the house, and Adam's car was nowhere to be seen.

She climbed from behind the wheel as the neighbour approached her.

'Hi, Kevin.'

'That bloody dog has been barking nonstop for the past fifteen minutes,' he snapped. 'I can't hear my television!'

Kay spun round to face the house. Lights shone from the downstairs windows, but the curtains had been drawn.

From the direction and timbre of the barking, Holly had been shut in the kitchen.

Then she saw a chink of light shining around the front door. It had been left open, the latch hanging at an unusual angle.

She reached into the car and withdrew the telescopic baton she kept under the driver's seat.

'Go back to your house, Kevin. And dial triple nine.'

'What?'

'Do it. Now.'

She closed the car door, and stomped across the driveway towards the front door, extending the baton and raising it to shoulder height.

She paused on the threshold, trying to calm her breathing, then assessed the situation once more.

Adam's car was gone; it was likely he'd shut Holly in the kitchen before going out, same as they'd done the past three nights before going to bed. On those occasions, Holly had never barked – Adam had made sure she'd settled on her bed, given her a pat on her enormous head and had closed the door behind him, safe in the knowledge that the baby monitor he'd set up next to her would alert him if the puppies were on their way.

The dog had never barked the entire time she'd been staying with them.

And the latch had definitely been smashed away from the front door with a heavy blunt instrument. Splinters of wood littered the doorstep, and the matching brass fitting hung from the doorframe.

Kay strained her ears to try and listen between Holly's barking, but she couldn't make out if the intruder was still in the house.

She edged along the hallway to the living area and peered around the door. The room was empty, but her heart sank at the sight of all their books, CDs, and films strewn across the carpet. The coffee table had been upended and lay on its side in front of the television, which had received a heavy blow to the middle of the screen. She emitted a shaking breath and then made her way upstairs.

Although the landing was well lit, all the bedroom lights were off. She snaked her hand around the door frame to the main bedroom until she found the light switch and held her breath, wondering what damage had been done.

The wardrobes had been emptied, the floor covered in clothing that appeared to have been stomped on. Her jewellery box had been discovered, but at first glance she couldn't tell if anything of value had been taken. The contents had been thrown across the room and scattered in all directions.

She gulped at the sight of her underwear flung over the bed, and resolved to throw all of it away as soon as possible. The en suite was empty, and as she made her way through the rooms it became apparent that whoever had done this to their house was no longer there.

At the sounds of sirens approaching, she made her way back downstairs and met two uniformed officers at the door. She recognised the older of the two, whose face broke into one of relief when he saw her.

'Hello, Norris. Whoever it was, we've missed them.'

'You should have waited for us, Kay. Where's Adam?'

'I don't know. Do you want to take a look around while I go and sort the dog out?'

Without waiting for his response, she made her way back through to the kitchen, opening the door while calling Holly's name.

The big dog launched herself at Kay and covered her hands in big wet licks. Kay ran her hands over her, but couldn't see that she was any worse for wear. She'd let Adam conduct a thorough examination on his return.

The sound of another car braking into a sudden standstill outside caught her attention, and she persuaded Holly to return to her bed.

'Kay? Are you alright?'

Carys appeared at the kitchen door, concern etched across her face.

'I'm fine. They'd gone by the time I got here.'

'I was on the way home when I heard the call go out. I recognised your address.' The detective constable looked over her shoulder at the two uniformed officers who had pulled on protective gloves and were now beginning to dust the smashed lock doorframe for fingerprints. 'What did they take?'

'I haven't had a chance to take a look yet. I was trying to get the dog to stop barking.'

'Adam's latest project?'

'Yeah. Puppies are due any day.'

They both turned as raised voices filtered through from the hallway, and Kay made her way out to the front door.

Adam stood on the threshold next to one of the uniformed officers, his face white.

'What happened?'

'We got burgled.'

'Holly?'

'She's fine – they left her in the kitchen. I've made a huge fuss of her, and she's calm now. Barking her head off when I got here.'

'I only left half an hour ago,' he said, his face distraught. 'We needed stuff from the supermarket. I thought I pulled the door shut properly.'

'You did. Whoever it was smashed the front door lock and forced their way in.'

Another car pulled up to the kerb, the driver killing the engine before launching himself from the vehicle.

Sharp shielded his eyes from the glare of the headlights from the uniformed car and hurried through the door. 'Are you both okay?'

'Hi, yes. We were both out when it happened.' Kay frowned. 'I must've missed them by minutes, though.'

Sharp craned his neck until he could see over Kay's

head and into the kitchen, as if he'd only then become aware of Carys's presence. 'Miles – I presume you heard it on the radio, too?'

'Yes, guv.'

'Alright, well if you're going to hang around for a while, I'll be off. Do you two need anything?'

'I don't think so,' said Kay. She reached out for Adam's hand. Colour was beginning to return to his face, and he'd finished checking Holly over.

'Just a bit of a shock to be honest, Devon,' he said.

'It always is. Right, well, I'll let this lot get on with dusting for fingerprints. Get a locksmith over. You'll be able to claim it on your insurance I presume?'

'I expect so.'

'Alright, well Carys here can help you make a list of anything that's been taken.' He turned, before he stopped and peered over his shoulder at Kay. 'Listen, why don't you come in a bit later tomorrow? Get yourself sorted out here first?'

'Thanks, guv. Appreciate it.'

He nodded, before hurrying back towards his car.

Carys turned to Kay at the sound of the engine starting. 'If you want, I can give you a hand upstairs while Adam keeps Holly company and sorts out downstairs.'

'Are you sure?' said Adam. He ran a hand through his hair. 'I mean, that'd be great, but if you have to be somewhere—'

Carys smiled. 'I don't, and we'll get it done faster if we split it like this, won't we? You two will still be trying to sort it all out in the early hours of the morning otherwise. I only have a decrepit gerbil at home who's on his last legs and smells of pee, so I don't mind spending a bit of time here helping you get things straightened out.'

Adam grinned. 'That's kind of you. In return, bring the old guy in to see me at the end of next week when I'm back at work. I'll give him a check over for you.'

'Deal.'

CHAPTER THIRTY

'Okay, let's see what they've taken,' said Kay, and led Carys through the hallway and up the stairs.

They checked the main bedroom and bathroom first. The duvet had been ripped with a sharp instrument – Kay suspected the same as what had been used to break the front door lock – and goose feathers littered the carpet.

'Looks like they made off in a hurry,' said Carys, her eyes travelling over the mess.

'I must've disturbed them when I pulled into the driveway.'

Kay moved to the doorway to the spare bedroom she'd been using as an office, and gasped.

She brought a shaking hand to her mouth.

The computer had been smashed to pieces, a gaping hole in the middle of the monitor where the screen had been shattered by the impact of something heavy hitting it. There was nothing left of the hard drive – that lay in tiny pieces, the edges catching the light from the spotlights set into the ceiling.

Worse, the boxes of baby clothes that she and Adam had so meticulously packed away and stored behind the door to deal with when they could face the task had been upended, the pink-coloured clothing tossed into the corners of the room while a blue soft toy rabbit lay in the middle of the floor, its innards tumbling from its stomach, bits of fluff covering the plastic mat under the office chair.

A gasp reached her ears, and she turned to see Carys leaning against the doorframe, tears in her eyes as she surveyed the damage.

'What sort of person would do this?'

'I don't know. I guess it could happen to anyone, right?'

She turned in time to see the younger woman's eyes fall to the baby toys and clothing.

'Oh, when?'

'Never, not now. Listen, Carys. No one knows, okay? Not even my own family. Adam and I didn't tell anyone.'

Carys's brow creased before she laid a hand on Kay's arm. 'I don't do office gossip,' she said. 'Never have. Hate it, in fact.'

'I know, sorry. I didn't mean—'

'Yes, you did. It's okay. If you ever need someone to talk to, say so.'

'Thanks.'

'Right.' Carys turned in the middle of the room. 'Where do you want me to start?'

'I think I'd like to tidy this all away. Do you mind making a start on the guest room?'

'I'm on to it.'

An hour later, Kay had re-boxed all the baby clothes away and placed the rabbit and its stuffing on the desk. She'd never been keen at sewing, but she swore she'd make an extra effort to return the toy to its former glory.

She'd moved from the unfinished office to the main bedroom, and took the opportunity to put clothes to one side that she should've taken to the charity shop months ago, and sorting the rest into piles of laundry that Adam would deal with over the course of the next few days.

Adam met them at the bottom of the stairs two hours later, a bottle of wine in his hands.

'This is for you,' he said to Carys. 'And when Kay tells me this latest investigation is over and you have time, come over and have dinner with us.'

'Oh, you don't have to do that.'

'We insist,' said Kay. 'And don't forget to take the gerbil to see Adam for his medical check-up.'

Carys grinned. 'I won't. Although he's almost a fossil now, you know.'

Kay waited with Adam at the front door while Carys got into her car, and waved her off as a van pulled up, a locksmith's logo emblazoned down the side.

'I'll let you sort him out. I'm going to finish upstairs,' she said.

She stood on the threshold of the office once more

and hugged her arms around her stomach, her thoughts churning. She heard movement at the top of the stairs, and then Adam's arms wrapped around her waist and he rested his chin on her shoulder.

'Can we salvage any of it?'

She flapped her hand at the boxes of baby clothing. 'I think so. They haven't done anything with this lot except throw it around the room. I can sew the rabbit back together.' She sniffed. 'He might be a bit lopsided though.'

He nuzzled her hair. 'You always make a joke out of things. It's okay to be upset.'

'I can't go there. If I don't hold this together, I'll probably fall apart.'

He kissed her. 'What did they get?'

She wiped at her eyes and reached into the pocket of her suit trousers, extracting a bright green USB stick. 'Nothing. Everything is on here.'

She turned in his arms.

'You were expecting something like this to happen, weren't you?'

'Not like this, no. But I—'

'What on earth did you do?'

'I logged into the database yesterday after everyone had gone home following the briefing.'

Adam's eyes flickered over her head to the trashed office. He swallowed. 'What did you find?'

'I'm not sure yet.' She held up her hand to stop him interrupting. 'Just a name. It might be nothing.'

'Might be nothing? Have you seen what they've

done to our house?'

A shaking sigh passed her lips.

'Come here,' he said, pulling her to him. He smoothed her hair. 'I'm sorry. I know this was my idea. I just didn't think – I didn't know it would be like this.'

'Nor did I,' she mumbled into his chest.

'Whose name was it?'

She shook her head. 'Let me rule it out first. I don't want to cast suspicion on anyone until I've checked it out.' She raised her head and ran her hands down his arms. 'How's Holly?'

'Calmer. I've been round and apologised to Kevin. He's fine – a bit upset he had a go at you, in the circumstances.'

'I'm just glad he didn't enter the house while they were still here.'

Goose bumps appeared under her fingertips and he shivered.

'They must've been watching. Waiting for a chance to break in.'

'They were lucky you put Holly in the kitchen.'

'So is she, I think.' He squeezed her shoulders. 'I've almost finished downstairs. You okay up here?'

'Yeah. I'll phone in a takeaway order in about an hour.'

'Sounds good.'

He kissed the top of her hair, then turned and retreated back downstairs. Soon, she could hear the vacuum cleaner humming and the hammering and drilling of the locksmith interspersed with a cheerful whistle.

She sighed, shook the bin liner until it opened out, and began to sweep the shattered pieces of her computer into it.

CHAPTER THIRTY-ONE

Kay dumped her bag under her desk, checked there were no messages waiting for her, and then wandered over to Debbie. 'Can you log out that phone of Nathan Cox's for me from evidence? I want to take it over to Grey at headquarters.'

'Sure. You leaving it with him?'

'For a while.' She waited while Debbie completed the paperwork before racing from the room.

Twenty minutes later, she pushed through the double doors to Kent Police headquarters and ran up the stairs two at a time, before hammering on a door that blocked her path.

Her security access wouldn't allow her to enter the digital forensics expert's lair unaccompanied.

Movement on the other side of the door preceded a face peering through the glass panel at her, a pair of intense green eyes framed by olive skin.

She held up the plastic bag and waved it in front of the glass.

The skin around the eyes crinkled before the face disappeared and the door opened.

'Hunter, what brings you here?'

'We've got a nasty one, Grey. Heard you were working here for a while instead of your usual haunt. I'm hoping this might help us.'

'Come on in and explain yourself.'

He gestured towards a pair of faux leather chairs next to a swathe of computer screens, which he expertly switched off with one keystroke.

Kay tried not to let her disappointment show; she'd always been fascinated by what Grey and his team were capable of, and he was one of the few who had stood by her in the aftermath of the Professional Services investigation.

'You know queue jumping is frowned upon around here,' he said, and held out his hand.

'Yeah. I know.' She passed him the plastic bag. 'But I think our killer's number is on that.'

He frowned, leaned over his desk and pulled open the drawer before extracting a pair of gloves. 'Explain.'

'That phone belonged to a man who was originally believed to have committed suicide, except it now looks like he was murdered – by someone who is still killing men of the same age group. Our lot can run searches on the phone records made to and from the phone, but we can't trace that withheld number. The killer drugs his victims and ties them onto the railway tracks, Grey, and he's been getting away with it.'

He arched an eyebrow. 'Until now?'

'Right.' She told him about Lawrence Whiting's murder, and the witness.

In response, he dragged the plastic bag away from the phone and press the power button. 'Dead.'

'It was on its last legs when I switched it on earlier.'

He pulled out the charger and plugged in the phone, propping it up against one of the computers.

'That'll only be five or ten minutes,' he said, and settled into the other chair to wait. 'Where did you get it from?'

'The mother of one of our victims – Nathan Cox. His mother said she couldn't bear to throw any of his stuff away. Originally, when I was there with Carys, I thought it'd be useful to go through so we could speak to the people saved to his contacts list, but then on the way back here I noticed there was a withheld number – someone called him a few hours before he died.'

'And you think it was your killer?'

She nodded. 'When we spoke to a friend of Lawrence Whiting's, he made a similar statement – Whiting received a phone call late in the afternoon. He wouldn't tell his friend who it was, and he went out to meet that person almost immediately. Within hours, he was dead.'

'You think they both knew who the killer was?'

'Or, the killer knew something about them and was

threatening them with that knowledge. Either way, it was enough to make them go to him.'

Grey leaned forward and pressed the screen of the phone. It flashed to life, the battery icon in the top right corner still showing red.

'What happened to Whiting's phone?'

'We don't know. It wasn't recovered from the crime scene, and it wasn't in his flat.'

'You think the killer took it?'

'Maybe. Whiting's number doesn't appear on the call register of that phone of Nathan's, so they weren't talking to each other.'

'All right. What you want from me?'

'Can you trace that withheld number?'

'Yeah. Should be able to.' He pointed to the blank stares of the computer screens around him. 'I'll have to fit it in around all this though.'

'What is it?'

His mouth twitched. 'Come on, Hunter – you know I can't tell you that.'

She smiled. 'Worth a shot. Okay, if you can find a number, and then let me know who it belongs to and where we might find him, that would be a good start.'

'No problem.'

'And if there's any more activity on it, can you call me? Doesn't matter what time it is.'

'Will do.'

He followed her to the door and unlocked it, but then placed his hand on the wooden surface and peered down at her.

'Was there something else you wanted to ask me?'

His green eyes bored into hers, a faint whiff of coffee on his breath.

Kay bit her lip, her thoughts returning to the search she'd conducted in the database the previous night.

Did he know?

Could Grey be trusted?

She forced a smile. 'No, thanks. That's everything.'

He dropped his hand. 'Okay, as long as you're sure?'

'Yes. Thanks.'

She pushed her way out into the corridor and hurried towards the stairwell, not stopping until she reached the landing between the floors.

Something in Grey's manner had changed during their conversation.

She had no doubt that he would help her in relation to Nathan Cox's phone, but what did he mean by asking her if she wanted help with anything else?

Was he implying he knew about her covert investigation?

He had worked on enough investigations behind the scenes to know if someone was trying to access information they shouldn't be, after all.

She glanced at her watch and sighed. It was only eight o'clock, and she was already exhausted.

'No wonder you're starting to get paranoid, Hunter.'

CHAPTER THIRTY-TWO

Sharp stopped talking when Kay entered the incident room and slung her bag under her desk before joining the group gathered around the whiteboard.

'Everything alright?'

'Yes, thanks.' She gestured to him to continue.

'Right, well as I was saying, we're now down to a reduced amount of administrative assistance on this investigation, thanks to an armed robbery at a pub on the Sittingbourne Road last night, so you're going to be responsible for your own paperwork for most of the time.'

A collective groan filled the room. Admin help was a luxury, and sorely missed when it wasn't available.

'Nevertheless, we maintain the same level of integrity as we started with. The superintendent hasn't approved overtime, but I know you want to see justice served to whoever did this to our victims. We carry on regardless.'

He drew the briefing to a close, and put the whiteboard marker pen on the desk next to him before he took a pile of reports Debbie West handed to him and disappeared into his office.

Kay rubbed at her right eye and tried to concentrate.

Her mind kept returning to the discovery that any mention of the missing evidence that had nearly ended her career, had been deleted.

She lifted her head and gazed around at her colleagues in the room.

Were any of them responsible for tampering with the system?

And if so? Why?

Was one of them somehow involved with the suspect they had been trying to investigate in order to arrest? Had they somehow protected him?

She wracked her brains, trying to recall if any of them had mentioned anything suspicious during that investigation, but she couldn't remember.

She sighed and dropped her gaze back to her work. She hated the thought of suspecting one of them. She despised the fact that someone was determined to stop her from conducting her own investigation.

Her fist clenched at the thought that her work had encroached on her home life. She had always sheltered Adam from the more unsavoury aspects of her job, and she sensed a shift in their relationship since the break-in last night, which frightened her. Yes, she'd been shocked and appalled at what had happened, but she wouldn't be scared off. Adam, on the other hand, enjoyed a relatively sheltered life. He hadn't been exposed to some of the experiences that she had, and she had to protect him.

She forced herself to try and relax; she couldn't afford to drop the ball on this one. No matter what was happening at home, she was responsible for helping Sharp to manage a murder investigation.

'Shit.' She read the paragraph of text before her once again, and then called out to Barnes. 'Ian, can you look at this?'

He pushed back his chair and wandered over to where she sat. 'What's wrong?'

'Take a look.' Kay handed him the page. 'I found it in amongst the documentation we got from the transport police. We hadn't looked at it before as we were looking for suicides. Check out the two names on the last page of the report.'

Barnes's eyebrows shot up. 'Same as two of the suicide victims,' he said.

'That's the connection,' said Kay, 'I'm sure of it. Not that rehabilitation programme.'

Sharp appeared at her elbow. 'What have you found?'

'Two years ago, at a set of points just outside Barming station, an engineering team were working on upgrading signalling. Alison Campbell was a graduate engineer; she was twenty-seven at the time. In total there were six people involved in the signalling upgrade who were at the scene when the accident happened. According to Cameron Abbott, when he was asked during the inquest, they had all undergone vigorous safety training and had worked on railways together before. Alison wasn't as experienced as the rest of team, but everybody had a soft spot for her and would look out for her as they were walking along a live track. That meant that trains were still running, although at a slightly reduced speed. They had been working since eight o'clock that morning and had taking regular breaks in accordance with health and safety regulations.'

'What went wrong?' said Sharp.

'Two trains had passed by during the previous hour before the accident,' said Kay. 'The team had posted lookouts several metres along the track where the crew were working and radio contact was maintained at all times. The alerts were provided to the team that a train was approaching and would be at their location within two minutes. As the train came into view, the crew moved to the side of the railway track, to wait for the train to pass. Although the track they were working on was closed, the track next to them wasn't – it was a precaution that they would leave enough space between them and the locomotive as it passed. Our victim, Lawrence Whiting, was one of the people tasked with acting as lookout. His role was to liaise with rail control via radio and warn the other team members when the train was approaching using a whistle and his voice. At the inquest, he was asked repeatedly if he had passed on every single instruction from the control room. The coroner asked Whiting if he was sure that he hadn't missed a last-minute message. Whiting maintained that he had passed on all information to the team as it was relayed to him. He was quite adamant that he had followed all the health and safety precautions set out by the railway company, and those the team instilled at the pre-start meeting that morning. Abbott said at the inquest that he'd turned his back to step away from the tracks, when Lawrence shouted to him and pointed over his shoulder. He couldn't hear what the man was saying, because the train was so close so he turned around, and stated that Alison was still standing on the track where they had been working. He called out to her to step away but he said she ignored him. As the train went past them she walked out into the path of it. He says, without a backward glance.'

'And both our suicide victims and our murder victim were present,' added Barnes.

'That's too much of a coincidence to ignore,' said Sharp.

'Right. That's what I'm thinking.'

'Are the other team members listed in the coroner's report?'

'Yes – Peter Bailey and Jason Evans.'

'Well, I guess now we know who our latest victim might be.'

'I'll make contact with the railway company and get details for both of them,' said Kay.

'Do that,' said Sharp. 'And if they give you any

problems, put them on to me. If we're right about this, we have another man walking around out there that has no idea he might be the intended target of a serial killer.'

CHAPTER THIRTY-THREE

With the investigation ratcheting up another gear, Kay had left a message with the railway company and then taken the cash Sharp waved at her and left the incident room in search of coffee for the team of detectives.

She made her way up Gabriel's Hill towards the café the team frequented, savouring the freedom from her desk for a moment. She often found her best ideas materialised when she was walking.

Her phone rang, and she rummaged in her bag before answering it.

'Detective Hunter? It's Doctor Williams here. You left a message with my receptionist the other day.'

'I did. Thanks for calling back.' Kay stepped under the portico of a deserted shop to get away from the busy pedestrianised street. 'We wanted to talk to you about Lawrence Whiting.'

'Of course. Dreadful business. I was shocked when I received your message.'

'Can you tell me why Lawrence was prescribed antidepressants?'

'He was struggling to cope after a colleague of his was killed in a train accident. As with most men of his age, he didn't seek help for a long time after the incident and tried to cope with his anxiety in his own way. I think a friend of his had a kindly word with him in the end. He was in quite a state by the time he came to see me.'

'Would that be the train accident in which Alison Campbell was killed?'

'Yes, that's the one. Lawrence was required to give evidence at the coroner's inquest. I think that's what tipped him over the edge. It was more than he could bear, to have to relive the experience in front of all those people and her parents.'

'We conducted a search of Lawrence's flat, but we didn't find any evidence of prescribed antidepressants. Had he stopped taking them?'

'The last time he came to see me, we discussed lowering the dosage. That was about six weeks ago. Lawrence felt he was coping better, and wanted to stop taking them immediately. I cautioned him against this, because it can be a shock to the system and I was worried about the side effects of doing so.'

'But he did so anyway?'

'Yes, he did. I had a follow-up appointment with him two weeks ago and I have to say I was amazed at the difference in him. He told me that he'd taken up yoga and meditation, after seeing some videos online about how it can help with depression. I'm not so sure about the truth in that, but it was helping him. He was eating healthier, and he was talking about joining a gym.'

'That's certainly the impression we gained from visiting his flat and talking to his sister. Our investigation has moved on considerably since I left my message. We've evidence to suggest Lawrence was murdered. When you last saw him, did he voice any concerns?'

'Not at all. It's terrible that someone who was managing to turn his life around so well should be taken from us so soon.'

Kay thanked the doctor for his time, and ended the call before continuing up the street towards the café. As she placed her order and waited for the coffees to be prepared, she mulled the doctor's words over in her mind.

She took the takeaway tray from the café owner, nodded her thanks and pulled out her phone once more as she pushed through the door.

'Lucas, it's Hunter. The traces of antidepressants in Whiting's blood samples? He hadn't been prescribed any six weeks ago. I've just finished speaking with his doctor. How long would it take for the drugs to leave his system?'

She listened to his response and then put her phone away and picked up her pace on the way back down Gabriel's Hill, all the pieces falling into place.

She burst through the door to the incident room,

placed the tray on Gavin's desk and spoke with him briefly before hurrying into Sharp's office.

'The killer has access to antidepressants. That's what he's using to drug his victims.'

Sharp turned away from his computer and gestured to her to take a seat. 'What makes you say that?'

'I spoke with Whiting's GP a moment ago. Whiting hadn't had a prescription for antidepressants for six weeks.'

'He could've got some from another doctor.'

'No – we didn't find any at his flat, remember.'

'Have you spoken to Lucas?'

'Yes – and he confirms the toxicology reports and everything points to a large dose of antidepressants being in Whiting's body at the time of his death, so our killer must have access to them somehow.'

'Any record of recent thefts from pharmacies in the area?'

'Gavin's running a search. I—'

She turned in her seat at a knock on the door, and Gavin stepped into the room.

'No reports on the system for pharmacy thefts of antidepressant drugs in the past twelve months, Sarge. Reckon our killer has his own stash of drugs?'

'Must have.'

'Along with a hefty proportion of the rest of the population suffering from mental illness,' said Sharp and ran his hand over his eyes. 'It doesn't get any easier, this one, does it?'

CHAPTER THIRTY-FOUR

Kay placed her hands on her hips, cast her eye over the details that had been added to the whiteboard over the past few days, and sighed.

'What are you thinking?'

She waited until Sharp joined her. 'We have a dead woman who walked out in front of a train, despite her parents and best friend stating she had no reason to do so. Someone has killed three of her colleagues, and we don't know why. According to the fiancé's neighbour, they were a happy couple and got on well with everyone.' She flung her hands up in the air. 'What the hell am I missing, Devon?'

'Have you managed to track down the fiancé?'

'Not yet. He's been a bit elusive; hasn't returned our calls.'

'Might he have something to hide, do you think?'

Kay rubbed at her right eye. 'I must be tired. I hadn't even thought he might be a suspect. Christ—'

'Don't beat yourself up over it. That's why we do this. Brainstorm. Talk it through, over and over until we get there. You're not going to be the one who gets the breakthrough every time.'

'I realise that, but even so—' She spun on her heel and raced across the room to her desk before shoving documents aside until she found the report she wanted. She returned to where Sharp remained next to the whiteboard and waved it at him. 'The coroner's inquest. When we phoned the mobile number the railway company gave us, there was no response on the one for Jason Evans – I've got a request in for the number to be traced to find out why, but look at this. The fifth member of the work team, Peter Bailey. For some reason, he wasn't asked to give evidence at the hearing, whereas his four colleagues were. We've left a message on his phone. If we're assuming our latest victim is Jason Evans, then every one of Bailey's colleagues who testified is now dead.'

Sharp checked his watch. 'All right, bring Bailey in. Get Barnes and Gavin to go and get him. Interview him formally, and see what he's got to say for himself.'

———

As Kay entered the interview room, a man got up from one of the hard plastic seats, a look of fright in his eyes. He wore jeans and a short-sleeved shirt, the bottom of a tattoo showing under the hem of the left sleeve.

'What's all this about?'

Kay held up her hand. 'Please, have a seat and we'll have a chat once we've completed the formalities.'

He ran a hand through his fashionably cut black hair, and then lowered himself into the chair. He leaned forward with his elbows on his knees, and waited while Kay and Barnes settled into the seats opposite.

Barnes hit the "record" button before formally cautioning Bailey as a witness, and then gestured to Kay to continue the interview.

'Mr Bailey, to get us started could you tell me what happened the day that Alison Campbell was killed?'

'I relive it every night,' he said, and slumped in his chair. 'I keep wondering if there's something I could have done to prevent it, but I was standing too far away from her when it happened. We'd been working on that piece of track for a couple of days. It was quite a short project, only three months in total to replace some cabling in the signalling. Alison had joined the company as a graduate engineer six months before, and she fitted in really quickly. All the boys on the team looked out for her. We were devastated.'

'I've got no knowledge of how a project like that works,' said Kay. 'Could you take me through how your day started?'

He shrugged. "We all got to site before eight o'clock in the morning. Lawrence was in charge of site safety, and always insisted on the safety briefing taking place on time. We'd run through the tasks for the day, double check everyone knew what their role was. If there was a formal direction from head office, that's when he'd communicate it to us. There wasn't anything that day though. So, we were out on the tracks by eight-thirty.' He paused. 'Surely all of this is in the inquest report?'

'It is, but if you don't mind, I'd like to hear it from you because I can only learn so much from reading a report.'

'Okay.' He took a shuddering breath. 'Well, the first part of the morning was business as usual. Rail control had closed the up line, that's the side of the two tracks we were working on, and were running trains on the other side of the tracks. Every time a train approached, rail control would radio through a warning, which would then be relayed to the team by the lookout. That gave us time to double check that no tools or anything had dropped onto the opposite track by accident, and finish what we were doing before the two-minute warning was given to move out of the way. We got a twenty-minute break at ten-thirty, and went back to the crew room. Everything was normal. Nathan put the kettle on, we grabbed our food from the little refrigerator we'd plugged in there, and sat around chatting.'

He ran his hand over his mouth. 'I keep trying to remember if Alison was acting any differently that morning. But she wasn't. There was no indication that there was something wrong. Lawrence called time, and we were back out on the rails just before eleven. Sometime between five past and quarter past, I can't remember exactly – you have to check the inquest report – we got the call from rail control that the next train was approaching. We had the doors to the electrical unit open as we were replacing one of the circuit boards. Alison seemed preoccupied getting the circuit board into place. I tapped her on the shoulder to get her attention to make sure that she'd heard the warning. She waved her hand over her shoulder at me and I told her to finish up what she was doing as we still had all day to complete the job. There was no rush. I began to check the live rail, and then Cam shouted out the two-minute warning. Alison was still working at the cabinet. I walked over to her and said, "come on, you can finish that in a minute, there won't be another train along here until half past". She dropped what she was doing inside, stood up and – I don't know – it was just a look in her eye, and if I'd known then what I know now—'

He wiped at his eyes. 'I turned and began to move into the safe zone we'd demarcated. I thought she was following me. I was already thinking about how we'd need to move the equipment up to the next control box after this job. You know what it's like when a train is approaching, you can hear the rails sing. Well, that started happening and then I could feel the train's approach through the ground. It was an express one so it wasn't hanging about. The smaller local ones would travel a bit slower, but the whole idea of the way we work is to make sure the trains are disrupted as little as possible. The train driver sounded his horn, which was a bit unusual because he would have been told we were working there and he would have known that rail control had already radioed through to us to get out of the way. Then I heard Lawrence yell and as I turned, I saw Alison lift her foot over the live rail. The train driver couldn't do anything. She didn't stop. She didn't look back. She just turned around, and faced the train head-on.'

A shocked silence filled the room.

Bailey dropped his head, and began to sob.

Kay stood up and moved across the room to him, crouched down and placed her hand on his knee. 'I'm sorry, Peter. I know that was hard for you, but I had to know.'

He nodded, sniffed, and pulled a cotton handkerchief out from his jeans pocket, then blew his nose. 'I know.'

Kay moved back to her chair, and picked up her notebook and pen once more as Barnes pushed a photograph across the table to Bailey. 'Peter, this is a picture of someone we're trying to identify. Do you know this man?'

Bailey's eyes travelled over the photograph, and his face paled. 'That's Jason Evans. What happened to him?'

'Jason was killed by a train two nights ago,' said Barnes.

'Peter, can you tell us where you were that night between the hours of eight o'clock in the evening and two o'clock in the morning?'

He jerked back in his seat. 'I was at home. Y-you can't seriously believe I'm responsible for killing him?'

'Can anyone vouch for your whereabouts?'

His brow creased. 'I ordered a pizza at eleven o'clock.'

'We'll need the phone number of the pizza delivery company.'

'What about between eleven and two?' said Barnes.

'I-I was asleep. I mean, after I ate my pizza – I sat up and watched telly for a bit longer, then crashed out. I had to be at work by six o'clock because that's when the delivery trucks arrive with the fresh food.'

'Going back to the day of Alison's death. You mentioned that there was no indication something was wrong with Alison that morning. The coroner's inquest stated that the investigation focused on it being an industrial accident, but it doesn't sound like that from what you've told us,' said Kay.

Bailey shook his head. 'They never called me to give evidence. I was a junior engineer at the time and, I don't know – I guess with everyone else being senior than me giving evidence, they figured I wasn't needed. But I said all along it wasn't an accident. She walked out in front of that train by choice.'

'Have you any idea why?'

'None whatsoever. It's gone round and round my head ever since. She and her fiancé were due to get married in three months. I remember when word got around at work; a couple of the admin girls organised a morning tea to celebrate. She seemed really happy. It was only that morning that I sensed something was wrong. She seemed preoccupied, which was unusual for her. She was so studious. She only mentioned to me the previous week that her manager had put her forward for their internal management fast track system. She had everything to live for.'

CHAPTER THIRTY-FIVE

Exhausted, Kay reached out and moved her mouse across the desk.

The computer screen sprang to life once more, and she cast a surreptitious glance towards Gavin's desk.

The young constable tapped a pen against his arm, his head bowed as he turned the page of the textbook at his elbow and then scribbled another note on the pad beside him.

'How are the exams going?'

He finished writing, leaned back, and put the pen down before rubbing his hands down his face. 'I know I shouldn't complain,' he said, a slight smile crossing his features as he dropped his hands into his lap. 'After all, I'll be working long hours like this when I'm a detective, but my head's spinning at the moment.'

'Give yourself a break. We're in the middle of a murder investigation, and you've already been sitting there for an hour and a half.' She returned the smile.

'You're not going to remember anything if you're tired. When's the next exam?'

'About four weeks' time.'

'Plenty of time to learn all that.'

'Yeah, you're probably right.'

'Are you going to make a move?'

'I think I might. I find I can concentrate on this stuff for an hour or so, and then my mind starts to wander. I don't think I'll achieve anything staying later.'

Kay turned her attention back to the news website on her screen, and forced herself to read another article.

She had to be patient. She couldn't risk Gavin becoming suspicious and wondering why she was so keen to get him out of the incident room.

She hadn't had a chance to phone Adam to tell him she planned to work late, but then she hadn't expected Gavin to stay behind and study. She glanced up at movement from across the room.

He was reaching under his desk, and then pulled out a bright-coloured backpack before shoving his textbook and notes into it.

'You driving home?'

'No – meeting some friends for a drink, so I'll probably get the bus or a taxi afterwards.' He shouldered the bag and made his way across to her desk. 'You staying here for a while?'

'Only for a bit. I won't be far behind you. Go on.'

'Thanks, Kay. See you tomorrow.'

'See you.'

She watched him move through the incident room,

his long legs clearing the space in a few strides, and waited until he'd closed the door behind him.

She glanced at her watch and began to count off the minutes.

She managed two.

Launching herself from her chair, she hurried over to Gavin's computer and exhaled when she saw that he hadn't logged out, and the computer screen was still displaying the icons for the various programmes they used.

Sharp had told him before about ensuring his computer was closed down before leaving the office. Even though the cleaners would avoid the room, and Kay would lock the door when she left, they simply couldn't afford anyone to see the progress of the investigation or tamper with any of the case notes.

Kay sent the police officer a silent thanks for his forgetfulness on this occasion, and eased herself into his chair, her hand hovering over the mouse.

She peered over the top of the screen to the open door. Somewhere in the building, she could hear a vacuum cleaner, and reckoned she had about fifteen minutes before anyone appeared.

The sight of the screen beginning to dim galvanised her into action. Her fingers closed around it and she moved the tracker across the desk to prevent the computer from going into sleep mode.

She hadn't a clue what Gavin's password was, and until she'd seen him yawning over his textbooks, she hadn't even known what she was going to do.

Now, a fleeting pulse of guilt shot through her.

She might not get another chance to do this, not the way the investigation would enter another phase and the detectives would have to take on extra work. The team would get split up soon, delegated other tasks on top of the Lawrence Whiting case, and she might not have the incident room to herself for much longer.

She bit her lip, before her thoughts returned to the state of the house after they'd been burgled, and the fact that someone was trying to scare her off.

If they were afraid that she'd stumble onto something, then she had to continue. It meant there was something worth pursuing.

But, what?

The noise from the vacuum cleaner drew closer.

'Now or never,' she murmured.

She clicked onto the icon on the screen for the HOLMES2 database and typed in the details for the case from memory. She swallowed, then hit the "Enter" key and twirled her ballpoint pen between her fingers while she waited for the display to refresh.

She wanted to double check the records for the evidence, the same record she'd seen last night. She couldn't go around pointing the finger and blaming other people, not without being absolutely sure.

She peered over her shoulder, paranoia manifesting in goose bumps on her forearms.

The office remained empty, and no one moved in the corridor beyond.

She swallowed, and turned her attention back to the computer screen.

The display refreshed, and the pen dropped from her hand.

'What the hell?'

She frowned, and peered closer, scrolling up and down the list of entries one way, then the other.

'That's impossible.'

She pushed the mouse away and leaned back in the chair. A chill ran down her spine, but she knew it wasn't because of the enthusiastic air conditioning.

Someone had removed all the records relating to the gun being recorded as evidence, including the name that she'd discovered only the previous evening.

It was as if it had never existed.

CHAPTER THIRTY-SIX

Kay changed gear, indicated right and swung the car into a rabbit warren of a housing estate early the following morning, and tried to keep track of the different cul-de-sacs disappearing off to her left and right.

'It's the second one on the right down here,' said Barnes, and pointed through the windscreen.

After concluding their interview with Peter Bailey, Kay had decided that she wasn't prepared to wait for Kevin McIntyre, Alison's fiancé, to return her calls.

Now, she pulled up outside McIntyre's house, and took a moment to take in the manicured front garden and tidy paintwork. A low privet hedge marked the boundary between the property and the pavement.

'What's the story with this guy?'

'Thirty-two. Currently unemployed,' said Kay. 'Hasn't returned to work since Alison died. Bailey said he didn't have to – both of them had life insurance, and so Kevin paid off the mortgage.'

'Nice one.'

'Except for the circumstances.' She unclipped her seatbelt and removed the keys from the ignition. 'Okay, let's go.'

She cast her eyes over the houses opposite as she locked the car, but it didn't appear that anyone was in. She checked her watch. It would be another hour before the schools emptied and the cul-de-sac turned into an unofficial playground within moments of the kids returning home.

She followed Barnes up the garden path, and waited while he rang the front doorbell.

'I don't think he's in.'

She spun around at the voice to her left, and saw a woman in her late sixties peering over the fence at her.

'Do you know when he might be back?'

The woman shook her head. 'Sorry, no. He doesn't go out that much; I only know that he's out at the moment because I saw his car leave.'

Kay beckoned to Barnes, and led the way over to the neighbour's house.

The woman stabbed a garden fork into the flower border as they approached. 'Is this about the deaths on the railway I heard about?' She didn't wait for a response. 'Did you know his girlfriend was killed on the same stretch of track a while ago?'

'I did,' said Kay. 'It's what we wanted to talk to him about.'

'It was awful. They were such a lovely couple. Alison always used to wave to me on her way to work, like she didn't have a care in the world. And they were due to get married in September. She had showed me photographs of the wedding dress she had chosen. They were going to go to the Dominican Republic for their honeymoon.'

Kay looked across the fence to McIntyre's garden. 'The house is looking tidy. How is he coping?'

The woman shrugged. 'He keeps to himself more these days,' she said. 'We don't see him as much as we used to. When Alison was alive we used to maybe go around there every couple of months for dinner, or they would come to ours. We used to have a cat, and Kevin would feed it if we went away. I think the last time I had a proper conversation with him was about three months ago, when he came around to help my husband cut some branches off a large tree we have in the back garden. It was terrible. He completely went to pieces after Alison died. We could hear him crying at night – the walls here are quite thin. We didn't know what to do. We offered to help him in the house and garden where we could, so that he had some contact with someone at least, but he simply wanted to be left alone to grieve. He really struggled after the accident, and then had to relive it all for the inquest. The investigation took ages. It seemed to drag out, when all he wanted was some answers. It was a terrible time for him. We were really worried about him for a while.'

Kay fished out one of her business cards from her

bag and handed it to the woman. 'We'd best be going. Thanks for your time. Perhaps you could pass that on to Kevin for me, and ask him to give me a call?'

'Of course,' said the woman.

'What next?' said Barnes as they drove away.

Kay tilted her wrist and checked her watch. 'We've still got an hour or so before the briefing this afternoon. The stretch of track where Lawrence was killed isn't too far from here – I want to go and take another look.'

It took her twenty minutes to navigate the car around the outskirts of the town centre and out towards the suburb where Elsa Flanagan lived. She drove past their eyewitness's house, and braked when she saw the gap in the fence and the start of the footpath Elsa said she had used to reach the field.

'Come on,' she said. 'Let's go for a walk.'

They made their way along the footpath, watching where they stepped amongst the muddy furrows in the long grass. They reached the end of the footpath after a couple of minutes, and it widened out at the top of the field. The railway line ran across the end of it from right to left, and to Kay's right she could see the steel gate in the hedgerow through which she and Carys had walked only a few nights before.

The field looked peaceful now, a small flock of starlings swooping over the far end before heading off across the railway tracks.

Barnes looked over his shoulder then back towards the railway tracks as an express train tore through the countryside. 'Whiting's killer must have waited until the other dog walker had turned her back to go home. I had a look at her witness statement – she didn't see anyone around at the time. She certainly didn't see Whiting on the rails.'

'In that case, he *must* have drugged Lawrence with the antidepressants. There's no other way to do it. He must have put him in the boot of his car or something, because Harriet said they definitely found dragging marks in the mud. They didn't get any footprints of the killer, so he must have covered the soles of his shoes.'

Barnes watched the last carriage recede into the distance. 'He got lucky, didn't he? There's only about twenty minutes in between these trains.'

Kay let her eyes fall to the twin tracks that cut through the landscape. 'He didn't get lucky, Ian. He knows this place. He knows the train times, including all the recent changes to timetables for the spring. He's been here before, even if Elsa Flanagan and the other dog walker never saw him. He's been planning this for a while, I would imagine.' She jutted her chin at the entrance to the field. 'It's what I couldn't understand the other night when we were attending the scene. Our killer isn't using this line to dispose of bodies.'

'What do you mean?' Barnes shielded his eyes as he stared at the railway.

'This is personal. He's making a point. I think that's why he made sure he only gave Whiting enough of the drugs to get him here. He wanted him to suffer.' She frowned. 'The question is – why? Why is this particular train route so important to him? And why kill Lawrence Whiting like that?'

Another train horn sounded from the direction of Maidstone, and a couple of minutes later a smaller three-carriage train sped past.

Barnes grimaced. 'Dave Walker said the trains only slowed by about forty miles an hour when they have people working on the track,' he said. 'I can't believe Alison walked out in front of one without hesitation.'

'Me neither,' said Kay. 'Which begs the question, why did she do it?'

'She certainly appeared to have everything to live for.'

'Exactly. So, what changed between the last time the neighbours saw her, and that morning?'

'Do you think she and her fiancé had an argument?'

'The neighbour said the walls in those houses are thin. I would have thought she would have said something to us if she'd heard an argument. But we'll ask McIntyre when we speak with him. It still seems pretty drastic though, doesn't it?'

Barnes kicked at a loose stone. 'All these deaths—'

'And not a single suspect,' said Kay. 'I know. I don't like it either, Ian. But, we keep digging.'

'I think we're going to need a bigger shovel,' he muttered, and trudged back towards the car.

CHAPTER THIRTY-SEVEN

The next morning after a fitful night's sleep, Kay slammed the car door and stalked across the car park to the secure entrance to the police station.

She had arrived twenty minutes ago, pulled up to the security barrier as usual and swiped her security card, only for it to be rejected. By the time she had roused someone to let her through the gate, she was already five minutes late for that morning's briefing.

The man who had let her through the barrier had tested the card for her and had handed it back with a rueful look on his face.

'You'll have to get a new one. The electromagnetic strip on this one isn't recognised in the system.'

Already tired and irritable from spending the early hours of the morning tossing and turning while she went over the case in her mind, Kay had cursed under her breath before thanking him and driving through the now opened gates.

She checked her watch. In all her years as a detective, she had never been late to a briefing unless she was out interviewing witnesses or following up another enquiry.

She reached out and pressed the button for the intercom, and then pushed the door open as the desk sergeant released the lock for her. He held out his hand as she approached the desk.

'I hear you've had a bit of trouble with your card. Let's get you a new one sorted out now.'

'I haven't got time, Hughes. I'm already late for the morning briefing.'

'Nothing I can do about it, sorry. You'll need a card to get through to the offices anyway.'

Kay groaned, handed over the now defunct card and waited while Hughes completed the documentation to issue her with a new one. She scrawled her signature across the bottom of the form he passed to her, took the card from him and then raced through the building, taking the stairs up to the incident room two at a time.

Sharp was mid-flow when she pushed the door open. He paused, and raised an eyebrow.

She held up her hand in apology, dropped her bag on the floor next to her desk and pulled up a chair.

'As I was saying before DS Hunter decided to grace us with her presence, if anyone hears from Gavin this morning let me know immediately. Right, today's focus will be following up on the information we've received from Peter Bailey in relation to the cause of Alison Campbell's death. We also need to speak to her fiancé as soon as possible, so keep trying his phone. I want to gauge his reaction to the outcome of the coroner's inquest. Carys, work with Dave Walker and Robert Moss from BTP to obtain copies of their reports following Alison's death. Cross check the witness statements against Peter Bailey's statement yesterday. Make a list of anyone else from those reports you think we need to speak to.'

'The inquest was held six months ago,' said Barnes. 'Alison died six months before that. I'm wondering why our killer only began after the inquest. If he felt that Alison's colleagues should have done something to prevent her death, why wait?'

'Maybe he was expecting justice for Alison from the outcome of the inquest,' said Kay. 'Perhaps the outcome was a shock to him – after all, everyone involved was exonerated. No one was held accountable, whereas he thinks they should be.'

Sharp tapped the photograph of Kevin McIntyre that had been pinned to the whiteboard. 'At the present time, until we speak to Kevin McIntyre and he provides us with some answers, he remains our main suspect. In the meantime, Kay – you and Barnes go and speak to the parents. It'll be interesting to see what they have to say about McIntyre. We'll reconvene at four o'clock as usual.'

Kay's desk phone began to ring as she wheeled her chair back into place.

'Hello?'

'Kay, it's Teresa in admin. About your swipe card?'

'Hi – thanks for calling me so quickly. I couldn't get into the car park this morning, and Hughes said something about the electromagnetic strip being damaged.'

'Yes, I don't know what happened there. We've checked it again, and it's not showing up in the system. It's like you don't exist.'

Goose bumps broke out on Kay's arms. 'Isn't that a bit unusual?'

'Absolutely. Normally that would only happen if we manually deactivated the card, for instance if someone leaves. I've spoken to my manager down here, and we've got no idea why this happened. I can only apologise for the inconvenience.'

Her mouth dry, Kay's thoughts turned to the previous evening. Had she somehow set off an alert while using Gavin's computer?

How else could she explain why her security card no longer worked? Was somebody trying to send her a message?

'Hughes said he's giving you a temporary card,' said Teresa. 'I'll sort out a permanent replacement one for you within the hour. If you want to pop up to collect it and I'm not here, I'll leave it with someone for you.'

'That's great, Teresa. Thanks.'

Kay ended the call and dropped the receiver into its cradle.

'What's the story with Gavin, Ian?'

'Didn't show up this morning,' said Barnes, glancing up from his computer. 'Sharp was pretty pissed off, I can tell you – especially when you were a no-show for the briefing as well.'

'Has anyone tried to phone him?'

'Yes. It goes straight to voicemail. I think all of us have left a message at some point for him this morning. Funny, I always thought he was a bit more responsible than this.'

Kay murmured a response and wiggled her mouse to wake up her computer. She entered her password, and tried to concentrate on the emails that had accumulated.

She tried to convince herself that Gavin was okay, that he was simply being an idiot and had ended up having a late night with the friends he said he was catching up with after work.

Except it was totally out of character for him.

A sickness began to churn her stomach and all sorts of scenarios began to go through her mind.

She tried to push her thoughts to the back of her mind, but as she stared at the computer screen and the words began to blur, she realised she'd soon have to stop thinking about her own investigation or else she'd be in danger of missing something. She had to prove to Sharp that she was capable of leading this enquiry. The incident of her swipe card had shaken her. Evidently, someone was trying to make her look bad. She couldn't let that happen. She glanced up, suddenly aware that someone was standing over her.

'Hey.' Barnes stood next to her chair and jangled the car keys in his hand. 'I said, come on, let's go speak to Alison Campbell's parents.'

'Sure.' Kay locked her computer screen, picked up her bag before grabbing her jacket from the back of her chair, and began to follow Barnes towards the door.

'Hunter, a word please,' said Sharp. He waved Barnes on, and turned to Kay.

'Guv?'

'What happened this morning? You're not usually the last one through the door.'

'Sorry. My swipe card wouldn't work. I couldn't get into the car park, or the building. I had to wait until someone could let me in. I've asked admin to look into it, and they've given me a temporary one.' She held up the white piece of plastic.

'All right. Get yourself over to Alison Campbell's parents. I'll see you at this afternoon's briefing. Don't be late again.'

CHAPTER THIRTY-EIGHT

Kay took a deep breath and closed her eyes for a moment, savouring the sun's warmth as she stood on the doorstep.

'Make the most of it,' said Barnes. 'They're predicting thick fog over the next couple of days.'

'That should make things interesting for our friends in Traffic.'

'Here we go.'

Kay opened her eyes and turned as the front door opened and a man peered out, his grey bushy eyebrows furrowing as he took in the two strangers.

'Martin Campbell?'

'Yes?'

'DS Kay Hunter. This is my colleague, DC Ian Barnes. We were wondering if we could talk to you about your daughter, Alison?'

He frowned, then stepped aside. 'Um, I suppose so. Come on in.'

Kay followed him into a bright living room, the fake cheeriness of the space tempered by the framed photographs that filled the length of an ornate mantelpiece halfway along the wall on the far side.

A gas fire sat in the grate where logs would have once burned, but despite this, a small collection of brass pokers hung from a rack to the left of the set piece.

Kay's eyes travelled around the room, and she nearly leapt back with a start when she noticed a woman sitting in one of the armchairs at the far end, her dark eyes peering out from under a mop of prematurely greying hair.

'Please,' said Martin Campbell, and gestured to the other armchairs. 'Have a seat.'

'Thanks.'

'DS Hunter is here to talk to us about Alison,' he said to the woman, before turning back to Kay. 'This is my wife, Karen.'

'Thanks for seeing me at short notice,' said Kay, and pulled her notebook out of her bag, aware of the couple's intense stares boring into her. 'I realise this will bring up some dreadful memories for you, and I apologise, but I'm interested in hearing from you what happened when Alison was killed. Where were you at the time?'

'I was at work,' said Martin. 'I had a job as a forklift operator at one of the big warehouses on Aylesford industrial estate.' He dropped his gaze to his hands clenched together in his lap. 'The warehouse supervisor came out of his office waving his arms at me to switch off the engine. His face was pale – I'd never seen him like that. I thought I'd done something wrong with the forklift for a moment, until he told me the police wanted to speak with me. They were waiting outside with the car – I could feel everyone staring at me as I walked across the forecourt towards it.' He swallowed.

'Mrs Campbell?'

'I was at work, too. I used to have a job then – at the garden centre near the motorway.' She wiped tears away. 'I haven't been back since.'

'Karen took Alison's death particularly hard,' said Martin, and reached across to take his wife's hand. 'I couldn't bear the thought of her returning to work until she was ready.'

'What was Alison like? I understand she was a very good engineer,' said Barnes.

'And to this day, I've got no idea where she got that from,' said Martin, a note of pride in his voice. 'Neither of us was any good at things like that. When we realised during her third year at secondary school how good she was at maths, we paid for her to attend additional lessons twice a week – she loved it. Soaked it all up.'

'Where did she go to university?'

'Plymouth,' said Karen. 'I didn't want her so far away from home, but she made friends easily, and we used to drive down a couple of times a year to see her, to save her coming all the way back here, and have a bit of a holiday together.'

'Is that where she met Kevin McIntyre?'

'No, she and Kevin met at a postgrad engineering

conference in Croydon a couple of years ago,' said Martin. 'It was a sort of careers convention – a lot of engineering companies had displays there so people like Alison could meet with them and talk about potential careers. After that, Alison was offered a job by the railway engineering company – their head office is at Dartford – and Kevin landed a job with a company working on the gas facility at the Isle of Sheppey. After that contract ended, he ended up working in their head offices in Ashford.'

'How long had they been engaged?' said Kay.

Karen pulled out a cotton handkerchief from her sleeve and gently blew her nose.

'About four months,' she said.

'Did she give you any indication that she was experiencing problems at home or at work?'

Kay caught the look that passed between the couple, and held her breath.

'You should tell her,' Martin said, and patted the back of his wife's hand.

Karen took a shuddering breath before speaking.

'I was in a rush to get out the door for work that morning,' she said. 'We used to have an old cat that we shut in the kitchen at night. When we came downstairs that morning, it had made a mess, so by the time I cleared that up, I was already running late. My mobile rang as I was closing the front door – the bus stop is a ten-minute walk from here. I saw it was Alison's number, so I answered it.'

'She was breathless, excited. It was hard to make out

213

what she was saying over the noise of the traffic beside me. I told her I couldn't talk right then, and that she should come over straight from work, and we could have a proper chat.' Tears rolled over her cheeks. 'And then within hours, she was dead. I never got the chance to talk with her again. I've always wondered what she wanted to tell me. I should've listened. I should've—'

Kay gave the couple a moment to collect themselves, and then frowned.

'What about her relationship with Kevin? Any issues there?'

'None whatsoever,' said Martin. 'Kevin doted on her.'

'Have you stayed in touch with him?'

'We drifted apart,' said Karen. 'It was so hard for all of us, but to then have to live through the inquest into the rail accident as well and with all the media interest – well, I'm afraid we became a bit reclusive. Maybe too much.'

'It was hard enough to deal with our own grief,' said Martin. 'We couldn't cope with helping Kevin through his as well.'

'What does Alison's death have to do with your investigation, Detective?' asked Karen.

'At the moment, I'm simply working with my team to investigate and learn about the deaths on that stretch of track, in the hope it might shed some light on our current enquiries.' Kay put her notebook back in her bag and stood. 'I appreciate you both speaking with me today, thank you.'

Martin eased himself off the sofa. 'I hope it helps.'

Kay shook hands with Karen, and then followed him out to the front door.

He opened it, then leaned forward and lowered his voice as Barnes headed towards the car. 'I appreciate you have a job to do, Detective. But nothing will bring our daughter back.'

His lips tightened, and then he closed the door quietly before Kay could respond.

She sighed, then stomped her way back to the car, her heart heavy.

CHAPTER THIRTY-NINE

Kay slipped through the door to the incident room and manoeuvred herself so she stood at the back, Carys joining her.

As the briefing commenced, she noted a subdued air amongst her colleagues and wondered what had happened during her absence from the office. Sharp finished speaking, passing on words of encouragement to the team, before he brought the afternoon debrief to a close, and everyone began to collect their belongings and head out the door for the day.

She frowned.

A distinct silence filled the space. Where normally the investigative team would be making plans to have a quick drink after work, or calling out to each other about the next day's assigned tasks, instead they seemed unusually quiet.

She grabbed Debbie as she passed her on her way out. 'What's wrong?'

'Gavin got beaten up last night. He's in hospital.'

'What?'

'Yeah. Couple of broken ribs, apparently.'

'Kay?'

She raised her gaze to the back of the room. Sharp gestured to his office.

'I'll see you tomorrow,' said Debbie. 'Plenty to do, right?'

'Right. See you.'

As she moved across the room towards Sharp's office, she heard Debbie and Carys leaving together, their voices fading as they walked away down the corridor, exchanging updates, and then she tuned them out.

'What happened to Gavin?' she said to Sharp.

'He was attacked in the car park next to the Bishop's Palace late last night. Apparently he'd been out for a drink with friends, and got jumped on the way back to his car.'

'He told me he was going to get a taxi.'

'I guess he changed his mind – he was certainly under the drink drive limit, as he'd only had a couple of light beers the whole time he was there.'

'Suspects?'

'Not at this stage. The investigating officers have the CCTV footage, although Gavin told them his assailants were both wearing scarves around their faces, so he couldn't provide any details.'

'How many of them?'

'He says two attacked him, but there was a third one

acting as lookout and driver – after they'd beaten him to a pulp, a car pulled up and his two attackers jumped in before it drove away.'

'How bad is he?'

'Two broken ribs, lacerations to his face. Bruising. They're going to keep him in for a couple of days to make sure there's no internal organ damage.'

'Motive?'

'None that we can ascertain – they didn't take his wallet for a start.'

Kay swallowed.

'Anyway, sit down for five minutes,' said Sharp. 'Bring me up to speed on what you've got to date. Anything of interest?'

'I've spoken with Alison Campbell's parents. Kevin McIntyre doted on her, but they've lost touch with him since her death.'

'Understandable, I suppose.'

'Yeah. Must've been terrible for all of them. Karen Campbell said that on the morning Alison died, she got a phone call from her as she was leaving the house to go to work. She said Alison sounded "breathless, excited".'

'Could that be mistaken for something else?'

'I wondered that. Karen said it was hard to hear Alison over the noise of the traffic – she was walking to the bus stop at the time. She told Alison to phone her after work.'

'Crumbs, that must be playing on her mind.'

'Karen hasn't returned to work since that day. I can't

imagine what she must be putting herself through.' Kay tossed her notebook onto the desk. 'I got the impression that neither of them are coping very well.'

'Did you explain the nature of our investigation to them?'

'Only that we have another case we're looking into at the moment and we were hoping to gain some insights into Alison's working relationship with her colleagues. I didn't see the point in raising the issue of Alison taking her own life – we only have Peter Bailey's word to that effect at the moment anyway.'

'Fair enough. We'll have to keep them informed if things progress and it transpires she did, though.'

'I understand.'

She pushed herself out of her chair and picked up her notebook. 'I'll chase up Kevin McIntyre first thing tomorrow. We really need to close out that angle and find out what he knows.'

'Agree.' Sharp switched off his computer and swung his jacket over his shoulders. 'Of course, it doesn't help we're a man down now that Gavin's laid up in hospital.'

Kay bit her tongue and followed him from the incident room, and then gestured to a door they were approaching. 'I'm going to duck in here before I drive home.'

'I'll see you in the morning, then.'

'Guv.'

She pushed open the door to the ladies' toilet, and placed her bag on the shelf above the row of basins.

She gripped the side of one of the sinks, and avoided looking in the mirror. She didn't want to acknowledge the guilt she knew would show in her eyes. Instead, she reached out and twisted the faucet, sending cold water gushing over the ceramic surface, and splashed her face before grabbing a couple of paper towels and pressed them against her skin.

She screwed them up and tossed them into the bin next to the tiled wall, and bit back the urge to shout with frustration.

Someone had found out about her ongoing attempts to find out the truth, and Gavin had paid the price for her stubbornness and refusal to quit.

She lifted her gaze, untied her hair and ran her fingers through it while her mind raced. She thought she was being smart, and that by covering her tracks she'd be able to shed some light on what was going on.

Instead, one of her colleagues was now convalescing in hospital, and she could no longer trust anyone else in the building.

Someone had found out about her logging in to the system to attempt to find out what had happened to the gun, and that same person appeared to be determined to send her a very clear message to stop – even going as far as deleting crucial evidence records from the database and attacking someone who had nothing to do with the vendetta against her.

She took a step back from the basin and shivered.

If she'd known she was putting Gavin in danger, she

would have never used his computer to continue her investigation.

She closed her eyes and bowed her head.

'Oh, Gavin. What the hell have I done?'

CHAPTER FORTY

Kay flicked her warrant card at the nurse sitting at the reception desk as she approached, and smiled.

'I realise I'm visiting out of hours. Could I see Gavin Piper, please?'

The nurse gave her a reproachful look. 'We have visiting hours for a reason, you know.'

'I'm sorry. We've been busy and I couldn't get away. How is he?'

'Sore, I would imagine. Two broken ribs, a broken nose, and a slight concussion. I hope you catch the bastards that did this to him. He's a lovely bloke.' She picked up a clipboard and handed it across the desk to Kay. 'Sign in. You can have fifteen minutes with him, no more – and that's only because he's got a room of his own and the doctor's already finished his rounds.'

'Thanks.' Kay scribbled her signature on the page and handed back the pen. 'Which way?'

She followed the directions the nurse gave her, and then turned and made her way along the magnolia-coloured corridor and past the opening to the main ward. Some of the beds had curtains pulled around them for privacy, while sleeping forms bunched up under blankets filled the other beds. An elderly man with headphones on spotted her and nodded.

She gave a little wave, wondering if he'd had any visitors that evening to wish him well, and then carried on towards the private rooms.

She checked the numbers on the doors until she came to the one the nurse had told her, and knocked before entering.

Gavin raised his head from the pillow as she entered and pushed the door closed, and she stopped dead, shocked at his appearance.

His nose had a large band of tape across it, bruises blossoming from each side and over his eye sockets. His usual neat blonde hair stuck up in tufts, and he exuded exhaustion. A nasty scratch scored one cheek, and he'd pushed down the sheets to his waist, exposing bandages wrapped around his middle. As her eyes returned to his face, she blinked.

He held her gaze, and then pointed at the bag in her hand. 'Please tell me you didn't bring grapes.'

'Hobnobs. Not the cheap imitation stuff, either.' She reached into the bag and waved the packet in the air.

'Nice one. Hand them over.'

'You'll be okay eating these?'

'Yeah. Luckily they only broke my nose, not my teeth.'

She smiled, and checked over her shoulder that the door had closed properly before reaching into the bag once more. 'I also brought these.'

She pulled out four miniature spirit bottles.

'Sarge, you're a legend in the making.' He tried to smile, but the movement brought tears to his eyes and he shifted uncomfortably in the bed.

Kay averted her gaze, looked at the television that hung from a bracket on the wall and noticed a football game was on. She wandered over, handed him three of the four small bottles and took one of the brandy ones for herself.

She passed him the packet of biscuits as well, then looked around the sparse room before striding over to the window and picking up the chair underneath it. She manoeuvred it until it was next to the bed and she could see the television.

Gavin held out the open packet of biscuits, and she took one before pointing it at the screen. 'Who's playing?'

'Real Madrid and Benfico.'

'Where are Benfico from?'

'Portugal. Lisbon-based club. Didn't take you for a football fan, boss.'

Kay shrugged. 'I don't mind watching the bigger games. Especially if I predict Barnes's team are going to lose. Again.'

Gavin chuckled, and then groaned and clutched his ribs.

'Sorry – I didn't mean to make you laugh.'

'It's okay. It happens if I sneeze or cough too, so I just have to deal with it.'

'You look a mess.'

He went to shrug, and quickly changed his mind. 'I've had broken ribs before. Snowboarding. Much prefer getting them that way to this, though. More fun.'

Kay leaned across and reached for the remote, turning down the volume on the game before turning back to him. 'What happened? Where were you?'

'I was with some mates at that new bar down on Bank Street, behind the Town Hall.' He blushed. 'They had a bit of a lock-in after the place had shut. Only a couple of the regulars and me, mind.'

'Fair enough.' Kay took another sip of her drink. 'Go on.'

'My friends left about half an hour before me. I got talking to the couple who own the place, and didn't leave until quarter to twelve. I'd left my vehicle in that car park behind the church and the Bishop's Palace that morning, so I walked back down College Road to get it. Bastards jumped me as I was entering the car park.'

'They were waiting for you?'

He gave a slight nod. 'Had to be. There was no one following me from the club.'

'How many of them?'

'Two – I might have been alright if I'd known they

were there, but they were too fast, and I wasn't expecting them.'

'You've filed a report and everything?'

'Yeah. Not that it'll do much good.'

Kay hesitated to agree with him, but what he said was true. It wasn't unheard of for people to be attacked in the town in the early hours of the night, and although many perpetrators were caught via CCTV footage, there were plenty that got away with it.

'Anyway,' said Gavin. 'Enough about me. What's happening with the investigation?'

She took a sip of the brandy before answering. 'We tried to speak to Alison Campbell's fiancé today but he wasn't home. It's sad; according to the neighbour, they were a really nice couple. Obviously, he's been in a state since she died, but the house looks tidy enough. We're waiting for him to get in touch with us now. I'll leave it until tomorrow afternoon, and if I haven't heard anything I'll pop round there again on my way home.'

They both looked up at a knock on the door.

'Give me that,' said Gavin, and snatched the brandy bottle from her hand.

The door opened, and the nurse that had been sitting at reception poked her head around it.

'I said fifteen minutes,' she said. 'It's been over thirty. I need to ask you to leave. He has to rest.'

'Thanks,' said Kay. 'I'll be out in two. Is that okay?'

The nurse nodded, and retreated.

Kay turned in time to see Gavin removing the two spirit bottles from under the sheets.

He grinned. 'Never took you to be one for subterfuge, boss.'

She took the bottle from him and drained it, before dropping it into her bag.

'You don't know the half of it, Piper. Get some rest.'

CHAPTER FORTY-ONE

Kay jumped as her desk phone rang, and cursed under her breath as the plastic water cup next to her elbow tipped over, spilling the dregs of its contents over a pile of manilla folders.

She reached out for the telephone with one hand, plucked a handful of tissues from a box next to her computer monitor with the other, and dabbed at the files.

'Kay Hunter.'

'Detective, it's Hughes on the reception desk. I've got a Kevin McIntyre here to see you.'

Kay screwed up the now sodden tissues and threw them into the wastepaper basket. 'I'll be right there.'

She grabbed her notebook and a couple of pens before making her way out of the incident room along the corridor and down the flights of stairs. When she reached the reception area, a lone man sat with his back to the wall in one of the plastic chairs that were bolted to the floor. Hughes, the sergeant on duty, looked up from his work and gestured with his pen towards the man. Kay nodded her thanks and made her way over to the seats.

'Kevin McIntyre? I'm DS Kay Hunter.'

He stood and shook her outstretched hand.

She took a step back, surprised at his height, and lifted her chin. 'Thanks for coming in. I'd have been more than happy to come by the house.'

'I had a dental appointment in town. I thought I'd pop in on my way home, to save you the journey.'

'Thank you, that's very thoughtful of you. Would you like a cup of tea or something?'

'No, I'm fine, thank you.'

'All right, well if you'd like to follow me, there's a room along here we can use.'

She led the way along the corridor and pushed open a door to one of the interview suites. She gestured to the table and four chairs. 'Have a seat.'

She waited until he was settled before opening her notebook to a fresh page and uncapping one of her pens, then explained the formal caution to him.

McIntyre leaned forward on the table and crossed his hands in front of him. 'My neighbour said that you wanted to talk to me about Alison's death.'

'That's right, I do. I'm sorry if this brings up painful memories. But I'm hoping you'll be able to help me shed some light on an investigation we're currently working on.'

'I still can't believe she's gone,' he said. 'It's almost

a year ago now, but I keep expecting her to walk back through the front door.'

'How well did you know her colleagues?'

He shrugged. 'I didn't know everybody that she worked with. There were three or four who she socialised with maybe once a month or so. Usually at a pub that was sort of halfway from where we all lived. We'd sometimes meet up on a Sunday afternoon for a couple of drinks, especially over the summer – Alison got hooked on an old pub garden game called bat and trap.'

'And how have you been, Mr McIntyre? Are you coping okay?'

He sighed. 'It's been hard. Lately, I can go a couple of days without thinking about her. And then I remember, and I feel guilty because I haven't thought about her. I can't imagine what it must be like for her work colleagues that were there when it happened.'

'What was your relationship with Alison like?'

'I beg your pardon?'

'Did you get on well all the time, or did you argue a lot?'

'We were due to get married in September this year. Does that answer your question?'

'All relationships go through a rough patch, Mr McIntyre. I merely wish to understand what Alison was like as a person.'

'We bickered from time to time, I suppose – same as anyone.'

'Can you tell me what happened that day from your perspective?'

'I was at work. It was about twelve o'clock. I was in a sales meeting with my boss and three colleagues – it was a telephone conference call with our sales office in Swindon. The receptionist, Annie, opened the door and I remember her face was really pale. She looked like she was going to be sick. She asked me to step outside the room, and my boss had a go at her for interrupting us in the middle of a meeting and she said couldn't it wait. I remember she never stopped looking at me. She told my boss it was about Alison, and that the police were in reception wanting to speak to me. I didn't wait for his answer – I left the room and ran through the building to the reception area. There were two police officers there, and they said there had been an accident on the railway. I asked if Alison was okay, and the female police officer looked at her colleague and then at me, and I knew. I knew she was dead.'

He wiped at his eyes, and Kay pushed across the box of tissues.

'I know this must be painful for you, and I'm sorry, but I'm investigating the death of four of her colleagues that were present when the accident occurred.'

McIntyre's head snapped up. 'What you mean? Nathan and Cameron killed themselves. That's what I'd heard. I thought it was because they couldn't live with the memory of that day. I thought it was because the antidepressants they were taking weren't working.' He blinked. 'Who else has died?'

'Lawrence Whiting and Jason Evans. We've reason to believe their deaths are somehow linked to your girlfriend.'

'Why?'

'It's the only thing that links the four deaths. One of the deaths is being investigated as murder, and that's when we became aware of the link with the other three men.'

'Why? What sort of monster would do that? Haven't those poor men and their families suffered enough?'

'Mr McIntyre, I have to ask as a matter of due diligence where you were on the nights of their deaths.'

His jaw dropped open, and then he recovered. 'I realise you're just doing your job, Detective Hunter, but I can assure you I was at home on those occasions. Since Alison died, I don't go out much these days.'

'Can anyone vouch for your whereabouts?'

He leaned back in his chair. 'Actually, yes.' He pulled out his mobile phone and slid it across the table to Kay. 'I've spoken to my mother every night since my dad died in a car accident two years ago, and I always call her when the nine o'clock news has finished.'

'You don't have a landline?'

A faint smile crossed his lips. 'Who does, these days?'

'And this is the only mobile phone you own?'

He frowned. 'Why would I want another?'

Kay pointed to the phone. 'I'll need your mother's phone number, please.'

CHAPTER FORTY-TWO

Kay hovered near DS Jake O'Reilly's desk while he finished a phone call, then met his smile with one of her own as he put away his mobile.

'Hunter – thought you were still snowed under with the Lawrence Whiting investigation?'

'I am,' she said. 'I heard you were looking after the assault case – Gavin Piper?'

'I tell you, I don't know what this place is coming to if an off-duty copper isn't even safe.'

'Any developments?'

'We've got some CCTV footage from the car park but the cameras all face the buildings surrounding it. There's only a bit of the car park visible. Looks like our esteemed councillors and town planners were more worried about graffiti artists tagging the walls of a medieval building than people getting back to their cars safe at night.'

Kay let the older detective carry on. She shared his

frustration, but realised that funding for cameras was often limited, and if the historical buildings around Maidstone were damaged instead, they'd be receiving the same amount of phone calls from the public. It wouldn't lessen their caseload.

'Could you see anything at all?'

He wiggled the mouse on his desk from side to side. 'Come round here and take a look for yourself. He's one of yours, right?'

'Yeah. Wants to be a detective. He's got the right attitude.'

'Well, hopefully this doesn't put him off.'

Kay swallowed, but said nothing. She hadn't even contemplated that outcome when talking with Gavin the previous night.

O'Reilly leaned over and pulled a chair across from the desk behind him and indicated to Kay to sit.

'Thanks.'

'I've taken a cut of the recording, so it'll save fast-forwarding. This starts off as Piper enters the car park.'

'Okay.'

He hit the "play" button on the screen and the black and white image juddered once and then the film began.

From the top right-hand corner, Gavin appeared, his hands shoved into his jacket pockets and his gait unhurried.

'This is his car, down here in the bottom left-hand corner. He parked under a streetlight, but the bulb had blown.'

'Convenient.'

'Yeah.'

She watched as Gavin reached the middle of the screen, halfway to his car.

Something caught his attention, and he glanced over his right shoulder before halting.

Suddenly, a man launched himself at the young police constable, attacking him from his blind side with a shoulder charge that gave him no time to take evasive action and sent him sprawling onto the asphalt.

Kay gasped, and covered her mouth with her hand.

She'd seen fights before, and had broken up a few in her time in uniform, but there was something utterly heart-wrenching about seeing someone she considered a close colleague take the brunt of an attack, even if she knew he was currently safe in hospital.

A second man appeared from behind Gavin, running into the frame before aiming a kick to his victim's back that made Kay's own kidneys clench in sympathy.

'Jesus.'

The two men bent down and began to punch him, aiming for his face and ribs.

Gavin curled into a foetal position, and tried to protect himself, but Kay knew only too well how that had fared for him.

He hadn't stood a chance.

She frowned as a vehicle appeared in the bottom right-hand corner at speed, and then stopped.

The two attackers' heads jerked up, as if they'd been called, and they rose from the asphalt, one giving Gavin a final kick to the ribs as he straightened, and then they both ran towards the vehicle before it sped off.'

'That's all we have.'

She blinked.

O'Reilly leaned across and stopped the recording, and then sat back in his chair and met her gaze.

'I couldn't see their faces.'

'We've tried enhancing it, but it's no good.'

'What about other CCTV cameras? Did they get the vehicle's registration?'

'Yes, but it didn't do any good. They were fake, and the vehicle was found burnt out in a lay-by up round the back of Boughton Monchelsea yesterday morning. An accelerant was used, and there are no prints.'

Kay sank back into her seat.

'I'm really sorry, Hunter, but I don't think we're going to have a lot of luck.'

'I know. There's not much to go on, is there?'

He shook his head.

'Okay.' She sighed and straightened before pushing the chair back under the desk behind him, and then patted him on the shoulder. 'Thanks for trying. Let me know if I can help with anything, all right?'

'Will do.'

Kay pushed her way through the door to the main corridor, and stopped.

To her right, the incident room awaited.

She checked her watch, and then turned her back on the hubbub of chatter from that end of the corridor, and headed towards the stairs.

She raised a hand in greeting to the police constables manning the front reception desk and pushed through the front door, before she shoved her hands into the pockets of her thin coat and turned left towards the river.

A cool breeze whipped at her hair and she peered up at the grey sky, wondering if warmer weather would make an appearance before the end of the month, or whether she ought to unpack her winter wardrobe again the first chance she got.

She pressed the button for the pedestrian crossing, felt a fleeting moment of victory as the traffic lights turned amber almost immediately, and strolled across the road.

The pavement curved as she passed the museum on the opposite side of the road and walked through the entrance to the car park.

As she crossed the car park, she narrowed her eyes at the spot where Gavin had been attacked.

A large seven-seater people carrier and a medium-sized maroon hatchback covered the parking bays where he had fallen, and as she raised her chin, she could make out the CCTV camera on its mounting next to the streetlight from which O'Reilly had obtained the video footage.

A chill ran down her spine and she stopped, before turning in a complete circle, her brow creased.

There was more than one person involved. She might have one name in mind, but there were others, that much was clear.

Was she being watched now? Were those that had arranged for Gavin's attack to take place spying on her?

She had no doubt that the men who had beat him up were not the puppet masters she sought.

The person behind all of this, the vendetta against her, and her subsequent troubles, was too sly and too intelligent to carry out such an attack themselves.

She shook her head to clear the thought.

Until she and the team had brought Lawrence Whiting's killer to justice, she couldn't afford to let her focus wander elsewhere. Somehow, she knew that time was on her side. So far, each warning had been reactive – she'd had to do something to provoke them.

Maybe if she waited and bided her time for a few days, they would think their ploy had worked?

'I'll find out who did this to you, Gavin,' she murmured. 'As soon as this case is over, I'm going to make sure they get put away.'

CHAPTER FORTY-THREE

Kay flicked the page and scanned the information that had been sent through from Alison's employers.

At first, they had been reluctant to assist, but after assurances that the police only wished to review the records for employment dates and any absences from work, a pared down version of her records was emailed to Debbie West.

'I've got the GP records here as well, Sarge,' she said, moments before forwarding an email to Kay. 'I've taken a quick look, but I can't see anything in there to indicate she might commit suicide.'

'There's no record of any problems at work, either. She doesn't seem the sort of person to act on impulse, which makes her walking in front of a train even harder to understand.'

Debbie pulled over a spare chair and sat down next to Kay. 'I guess it would depend on what she and Kevin McIntyre had an argument about.'

'You're right, but even so—'

'Seems a bit drastic, doesn't it?'

'Yeah, exactly. And she doesn't come across as being a drama queen.' Kay flicked through her notes. 'How far along were they with planning the wedding? Here it is – they announced their engagement three months before she killed herself. The wedding was meant to take place in September this year.'

She closed her notebook and grabbed her mobile phone from the desk, before dialling Martin Campbell's number. 'Let's find out what her bridesmaids have to say about her. Hello? Mr Campbell? Yes, I wonder if you could help me.'

———

'So how come you're dragging me along to this, and not our protégée?'

Kay tossed the car keys to Barnes and swung herself into the passenger seat. 'Because if I take Carys, I'll have to listen to how well she's managing her case load and why I'm supposedly throwing advantages Gavin's way and not hers, despite him being in hospital at the moment.'

The older detective smiled as he steered the car out of the police station car park. 'You can't fault her ambition. She's good.'

'They both are, and I've got a lot of time for them, but sometimes even your bad sense of humour can be appealing.'

'Aw, Sarge, you're making me blush.'

'Don't push it.'

They laughed, and Kay pulled out her notebook to share what she'd gleaned from Alison's father about the woman who had been picked by his daughter to be her matron of honour.

'Okay, so Rebecca Ashgrove. Twenty-seven, married with a one-year-old son. We're on a tight schedule as she has to leave before two o'clock so she can go and pick him up from day care. She's over at Wateringbury.'

'Right.' Barnes aimed the car over the River Medway and they picked up speed once they were out of the town's speed limits. 'Any more?'

'According to Alison's father, she didn't want a whole bunch of friends queuing up to be bridesmaids, so she only had the one.'

'Makes our job easier.'

Rebecca Ashgrove opened her front door and admitted the two detectives with the hurriedness of a mother of a new-born, and Kay was immediately struck by the smell of nappies and baby food.

No matter what new parents said, it clung to everything, and Kay pushed aside the sense of longing that threatened to overwhelm her. Instead, she cast her eyes around the living room, noting the careful placement of sharp objects or delicate ornaments, and turned to see Rebecca smiling at her.

'It's a whole new world, like, having Elizabeth in our lives,' she said, and moved a small collection of soft toys from the sofa so they could sit down. 'So I'm not going to even apologise for the mess.'

'It's not a problem,' said Kay. 'It's got a happy feel in this room.'

Dimples appeared at the corners of the woman's mouth. 'It has, right?' Her face grew serious. 'But you're not here to talk babies, are you?'

'We were wondering if you could help us with an investigation. Some background information, if you can, with regard to Alison Campbell. Can you tell us a bit about her? How long had you known her?'

Rebecca settled back into an armchair and curled her legs up underneath her. 'We'd known each other since secondary school, like, forever. You know what it's like – a whole bunch of kids from different villages all getting thrown together aged twelve in one big school. I think both of us had eyes like saucers the first day, like, we didn't know what to do, or where to go. We just gravitated towards each other, y'know? When we left school, Alison went off to university to study engineering, and I decided to study floristry. By the time Alison graduated, I had my own shop in Maidstone. She used to come in, like, and help me during her semester breaks.'

'Did she enjoy that?'

'She was a right laugh – she made even the dull jobs fun. We'd often take longer to clear up or do the stocktake every week just to gossip, like, y'know?'

Barnes finished writing. 'Any indication that she might have been depressed?'

'No, none at all. Trust me, I keep thinking back to the days before she died, wondering if I should've picked up on something, but there's nothing.'

'We understand that she and Kevin might have had an argument the morning before she died,' said Kay. 'Do you know anything about that?'

'First time I've heard about it. Kevin's never mentioned it.'

'Do you stay in touch with him?'

She shook her head, before her eyes dropped to her lap and she twisted the wedding band on her finger. 'No. I only knew him through Alison, so to be honest it wasn't hard to drift apart after she died.' She raised her head and shrugged. 'Alison was my best friend. I didn't even think to stay in touch with Kevin afterwards.'

Back in the car and travelling back to Maidstone, Kay bumped her fist against the car window and mulled over Rebecca's comments.

Despite the woman's assertion she and Alison had been best friends, it didn't sound as if Alison trusted her enough to talk to her about what was troubling her so much that she thought her only option was to kill herself.

What could have been troubling the young graduate engineer? Had she made a mistake at work? Who held her colleagues responsible for her death?

'I think I'd better give her employers another call when we get back to the incident room, Ian. We've only seen what's on her official personnel file. Maybe there was something else going on there.'

'I've been thinking that, too. I'll get in touch with McIntyre's employers as well. That might unearth something of interest, you never know.'

'You don't mind? You've got Rebecca's statement to type up as well.'

Barnes shook his head. 'Shouldn't take long. By the time I've omitted the word "like", this statement's only going to be a half a page, anyway.'

CHAPTER FORTY-FOUR

He ended the call and flung the mobile phone across the room in a fit of rage. The man had refused to meet with him, despite his best attempts to entice him away for a quiet chat, as he had put it.

His hands shook and as he turned to pick up the glass of water next to him, he caught the scent of his own unwashed body and clothes. He had managed to hold himself together so that when he spoke with the police, they wouldn't suspect anything. But now, as the ending drew near and his project delivery programme drew close to its foregone conclusion, his own hygiene had fallen away.

He tried to regain control, pushing down the anger with the large gulp he took before replacing the glass on the table.

He couldn't afford to draw attention to himself. Until now, he had worked without interruption. Despite the unfortunate events involving the dog walker, he had regained his confidence in his abilities to deliver his projects on time. He was further emboldened following his conversation with the police.

They had no idea who was carrying out the killings, that much was clear.

He clenched his fists.

He reached for his diary – the one he completed each night in careful handwriting using a soft pencil and neat, precise sentences. It sometimes took an hour or two to note down all his thoughts and plans, but there was no rush. There was nowhere else he needed to be.

Afterwards, he would take an eraser and rub out all trace of his meanderings. The words weren't important; what mattered was getting them onto the paper and out of his mind.

When Alison had died, his doctor had told him that keeping a diary might help him cope with his grief. It had turned into so much more than that. Sometimes he would write for what seemed an age, and then stop and read what he had written. The words often surprised him. He didn't know where they came from, but he recognised the frustration and anger they held.

He placed the pencil between the pages and closed the journal. He hadn't finished yet – his mind still somersaulted – but the words hadn't yet formed. He had learned over the past months to take his time. He ran his hand over the embossed leather cover and sniffed before rubbing at his eyes with a knuckle. Alison had bought the journal for him for his birthday the previous year. She alone understood his busy mind.

His chest ached with the pain of losing her. His throat tightened, and another wave of tears threatened, his eyes stinging. He didn't believe the heartache would leave him, not ever, despite the kind words his doctor had conveyed as he'd thrust a handful of sombre-coloured brochures at him with titles such as "Understanding Grief".

He understood grief, all right.

It was savage; all-consuming. Every waking moment was spent wondering what it would be like now if she were still alive.

He reopened the journal, the page blurring as he continued to write despite the tears that tracked down his cheeks. Sometimes, it was almost as if he was talking to Alison directly, as if she would hear the words he set down.

He could imagine her, her head leaning to one side as she always did when she concentrated on what was being said to her. She'd wait until the person had finished speaking, wait a couple of seconds, and then her eyes would light up and the debate would begin.

What if? Why not? And how could they?

His mind at rest, he set aside the journal once more.

His thoughts turned to the metal toolbox he kept under the table that held the model railway. Crouching down, he flipped open the lid, removed the inner tray, and pulled out the bottles of pills he had been saving. He straightened, and unscrewed the lid of the bottle. Tipping out the contents into the palm of his hand, he counted the number of pills that remained.

He didn't have many; the keys he'd found in Lawrence Whiting's pocket had slipped easily into the lock of the door to the man's flat, and a quick search of the bathroom cabinets had revealed a half-used prescription for the antidepressants. He had worn gloves, like he'd seen the police wear on television and made sure not to touch anything else in the flat before retreating and quietly shutting the door behind him.

He reached for his notebook and pen, where he had jotted down his estimate for Peter Bailey's weight after following the man home from work earlier that week.

He had hung back in the shadows, convinced that the man knew he was being followed. He checked the dosage against the man's weight. No matter what Bailey said, he had to meet with him.

He had to find a way.

There were enough pills to complete the final project, as well as enough for him. He tipped the pills back in the bottle, tightened the screw cap, and returned them to the toolbox.

He flicked a page in his notebook. And as he did so, his eyes fell upon the framed photograph he'd arranged next to the model railway controls.

He had done all of this for her. It was their fault she had been taken from him so early. They should have been looking out for her. They had always told him she was like a little sister to them, so why didn't they look out for her and keep her safe from harm?

CHAPTER FORTY-FIVE

The sound of Barnes's fingers tapping away on his keyboard provided the perfect white noise for Kay as she sifted through the information they'd received from both Alison and Kevin's employers.

She'd spend half an hour speaking with her insurance company about the break-in upon their arrival back at the incident room.

By the time she'd been put on hold three times and then jumped through all the hoops to arrange for an assessor to visit and for a copy of the police report to be sent in to them in order for her claim to be processed, the afternoon light had faded and she was relieved to return to her work.

'Interesting.'

'What've you got?'

Barnes tapped his screen. 'As part of Kevin's employment package when he started with the engineering company, he was provided with a mobile phone. Says here that it was never returned.'

'He never mentioned a second phone when I interviewed him.'

'Now, why would that be?' Barnes raised an eyebrow.

Kay checked her watch. The afternoon briefing was due to start in five minutes. 'Only one way to find out. I'll phone him and ask.'

She drummed her fingers on the desk while the number connected and then rang, before giving up when it went to voicemail. She shook her head and disconnected. 'No answer. Do you have the number there for the work mobile?'

Barnes read it out to her, then peered over her head. 'Looks like Sharp's about to start the briefing.'

'Won't be a minute.' Kay keyed in the numbers for the second mobile phone and waited.

Again, the call connected but this time went straight to voicemail.

'Can't be charged up,' she said.

'You need to see this, Sarge.'

Kay looked up from the mobile phone at the sound of Carys approaching. 'What've you got?'

'I thought I'd do another search for Kevin McIntyre to finalise the statement we have from him. Take a look at this.' She handed over the document. 'It's a record of a phone call Cameron Abbott made to the desk duty officer the week before his death. '

'Why's it taken until now to find this?'

'His name didn't turn up when we ran the searches on the database earlier this week, because it's been spelled differently in this report.'

'What did Abbott report?'

'Cameron said that McIntyre was harassing him – phone calls, following him, threatening him. McIntyre had a different mobile number at the time. He was cautioned, but nothing else. Cameron died three days later.'

———

Kay hung on to the strap above the passenger door as Barnes slewed the car around a mini roundabout and accelerated once more.

In her other hand, she held her mobile phone, relaying instructions to Carys to organise the nearest patrol car to meet them at McIntyre's address with a search warrant.

Her seatbelt dug into her chest as Barnes braked outside the house, and she ended her call.

'Are you absolutely sure about this?'

'Yes. It all makes sense. He blames everyone on the project team for Alison's death. He refused to accept the coroner's findings at the inquest, and couldn't accept that she killed herself. He still believes that they should have done something to save her.'

'You think the outcome of the inquest tipped him over the edge?'

Kay nodded. 'Yeah, I do.'

She launched herself from the car and strode towards the house, pushing open the garden gate.

Seconds later, she hammered on the door despite the fact that she'd already rung the doorbell three times with no response. 'Where the hell is he?'

'The bastard,' said Barnes. 'He was fooling us all along. How the hell did we miss it?'

Kay ignored him and rang the doorbell again, keeping her finger pressed on the button as a series of chimes echoed through the hallway beyond the door.

'Do you want me to try to pick the lock?'

'No – we need the warrant, and it'll be quicker to break it down anyway.'

She brushed past Barnes and stepped over to the front window. The orange glow of the streetlights reflected in the glass, and she leaned forward holding up her hand to shield her eyes and tried to peer into the house.

Net curtains prevented her from seeing into the room, and she cursed under her breath.

She turned and surveyed the darkened street, wondering what to do next.

She was about to ask Barnes where the hell the uniformed patrol were so they could break down the door, when she heard footsteps approaching. She spun round on her heel to see the next door neighbour hurrying up the garden path.

'Can I help you?'

'Do you know where Kevin is?'

'No, I'm sorry – I don't. I haven't seen him for a few days. He was looking a bit run down.'

Barnes snorted at the unfortunate turn of phrase, and Kay glared at him before turning back to the neighbour.

'When was the last time you saw him?'

'I think it was two days ago. I'm glad you're here. I was starting to get worried about him.'

A police car, its blue lights ablaze, screeched to the kerb and two uniformed officers climbed from the vehicle before hurrying towards them. One of them carried a battering ram; the other handed her the executed warrant.

'At last,' said Kay. She checked the warrant before pointing at the front door. 'Get us in there.'

The neighbour's eyes opened wide. 'Wait – I think I've got a front door key somewhere.'

'Hurry – go and get it.'

Barnes paced the paved area in front of the front door, and Kay tried to ignore the itching in her right eye while they waited. After a couple of minutes, the police officer with the battering ram raised an eyebrow.

'Shall I?'

Kay sighed, and checked her watch. As she was about to give the order, the neighbour appeared at the garden gate and hurried towards her.

'I found them. Here you are.'

Barnes held out a pair of gloves to Kay. She pulled them over her fingers before taking the keys from the neighbour and inserting one into the lock.

The door swung open easily. She kicked aside three envelopes from the doormat, and called over her shoulder.

'Barnes, you're with me. Everyone else, stay outside.'

CHAPTER FORTY-SIX

The first thing Kay noticed was the smell. It was as if her nose and throat were being assaulted. The stench of rotting food, unwashed clothing, and a blocked drain filled her senses.

'No wonder he wanted to come to the station to speak with us,' said Barnes. 'This place is a dump.'

The neighbour gasped from her position on the doorstep. 'I had no idea. What's wrong with him? Is he all right?'

Kay didn't respond, and instead pushed open the door to her right. It led into a medium-sized living room, which hadn't been cleaned for months. Being careful where she trod, she began a slow route around the edges of the room first, her eyes roaming over the dusty bookshelves, the television that didn't look like it had been switched on in weeks, and the various coffee mugs that had been left to moulder on different surfaces.

Takeaway boxes littered the floor, together with an

assortment of soft drink cans that had been crushed in the middle and tossed onto the stained carpet.

She moved closer to a set of silver-framed photographs on one of the shelves, and peered at the images.

In one, McIntyre stood with his arms around Alison Campbell, huge smiles on their faces. Kay's eyes were drawn to the large engagement ring on Alison's left hand, before she swept her eyes over the other three photographs.

'These must've all been taken to mark their engagement,' she said, and pointed to each. 'Professional photographer, too, I would imagine.'

Barnes peered over her shoulder. 'He's fallen apart, hasn't he? I can't imagine it looked like this when Alison was alive.'

Kay murmured her agreement. She'd seen it before – a grief-stricken spouse or partner who retreated into themselves over time, gradually withdrawing from society and not caring whether they ate or slept.

She'd never seen someone actively create two lives for themselves though, not to this extreme. The time and effort McIntyre had gone to in order to give the impression to his neighbours and to the police that he was functioning normally had provided an effective smokescreen from the reality of his existence.

'Kay, you need to see this.'

She turned to where Barnes was standing with his hands in his pockets next to the coffee table, his head bowed.

Kay leaned over and picked up a manilla folder covered in coffee stains. Opening the flap, she tipped out the contents onto the low table.

'Photographs.'

They crouched and began to sift through the pictures.

Level crossings, platforms, pedestrian crossings, footpaths beside railway cuttings and footbridges over rail lines flickered before Kay's eyes.

'This is an obsession,' she murmured.

'Here. Timetables. He's highlighted the express services, look.'

Kay traced her finger down the page. 'And the last service.'

'Ties him to Jason Evans' murder.'

Barnes dropped the timetables and pointed at the documentation spread across the rest of the table. 'Maps, calculations.' He leaned down and picked up a notebook and began to leaf through the pages, before stopping and holding it up to Kay. 'I think we've found our killer.'

'I think you're right.'

'We need to tell Sharp.'

Kay's heart lurched, and she grabbed the sleeve of Barnes's jacket and began to drag him from the room.

'What's wrong?' he said, as he stumbled to keep up with her.

They reached the front door and Kay gestured to the two uniformed officers waiting on the doorstep.

'You two stay here. No one enters until the CSI team

get here.' She pulled Barnes down the garden path towards the car.

'Where are we going?' he said.

She stopped, and let go of his arm. 'We need to make sure Peter Bailey is okay. We have to make sure McIntyre hasn't got to him first.'

Kay hammered her fist against the front door of Peter Bailey's flat a second time, cursing under her breath.

McIntyre had managed to fool them all, and as she'd stormed up the stairs to the third-floor flat, she'd wondered what she'd have done differently given another chance.

She knocked again, then put her ear to the door.

Silence.

'Out of the way. We don't have time to wait for another uniform patrol to get here. I'll use my lock picks,' said Barnes.

'Hurry, Ian. I don't like this.'

He pursed his lips before crouching in front of the lock and extracting a leather pouch from the inside of his jacket. He withdrew two picks, sized them up against the lock, and set to work.

Kay paced impatiently behind him, her mobile phone to her ear while she brought Sharp up to date so he could organise the rest of the team, and tried to ignore the distinct marijuana fragrance escaping from underneath the door opposite to the one Barnes worked on.

Right now, her priority was finding Peter Bailey.

A door slammed at the end of the corridor and a woman edged towards them, an anorak pulled down low over blue jeans, her face hidden by a headscarf and her eyes wary at the sight of two strangers trying to break into her neighbour's flat.

Kay ended her call and pulled out her warrant card. 'Do you have a spare set of keys to this flat?'

The woman shook her head before lowering her eyes and hurrying past.

'Friendly neighbourhood,' muttered Barnes.

'Would've been too easy.'

'Here we go.'

He straightened, and turned the handle.

The front door opened into the living area, the light from the communal hallway pooling over a threadbare green carpet.

'Peter? It's DS Hunter from Kent Police. Are you in here?'

When she received no response, she nodded to Barnes and pulled on a pair of gloves. In the soft orange light from a streetlight outside the front window, her immediate thought was that the room was sparsely furnished and in desperate need of a new coat of paint. Her next thought was that the whole atmosphere held the air of a life in limbo.

She sniffed, the scent of recent cooking activity wafting from the direction of a small kitchen off to one side of the living room.

'I'll take the bathroom and bedroom.'

'Okay.'

Kay waited until Barnes had disappeared through a low arch that separated the rest of the flat from the living area before she moved past a low coffee table and cast her eyes over the papers laid across its surface. She sifted through the motorbike magazines and a holiday brochure from one of the local travel agencies, but found nothing to indicate where Bailey could be.

Next, she pulled the cushions off the sofa, grimacing at the age-old pizza crumbs and other detritus that had fallen between the cracks, before tossing them to one side and moving through to a small kitchenette off to the side of the living area.

A four-pack of beer stood next to the toaster, a scattering of crumbs around its base, while the outer wrapping for a microwave meal had been left on the worktop nearer the refrigerator.

Kay opened it, scanned the meagre contents, and slammed it shut with a sigh of exasperation before popping the door open on the microwave. A plastic dish containing what appeared to be a lasagne had been left on the glass turntable. She reached out and held her finger to the cellophane surface.

It was still warm.

Wherever Bailey was, he'd left in a hurry.

'We must've missed him by minutes,' she muttered.

She closed the microwave and began to check the cupboards – people hid things in strange places, and she knew better than to discard any ideas before conducting a thorough search.

Finally satisfied, she left the room and saw Barnes cross the hallway from the bathroom to the bedroom.

'Anything?'

'Not yet. You?'

'No.'

She let out an exasperated sigh, and then pulled her phone from her bag as it began to ring.

'Guv?'

'Status?'

'We're in the flat. No sign of Bailey. We're still searching.'

'I've arranged for a uniform car to attend. If necessary, they'll stay on site once you've finished conducting your search.'

'Thanks.' Kay swallowed. It seemed she wasn't the only one thinking the flat may well have to be declared a crime scene if they didn't find the occupant safe and well. 'We're nearly done here. I'll call you back in a bit with another update.'

Kay's phone vibrated, and she put it to her ear once more. 'Grey? I'm a bit busy right now.'

'Your mystery mobile number went live thirty minutes ago. He rang someone. Do you recognise this number?'

She froze as she listened, the digits tumbling over in her head. The sequence sounded familiar, but she couldn't place it. Dread began to creep through her veins, increasing her heart rate as an idea began to form. 'Call Carys. See if it matches anyone on our database.'

'Will do. I'll call you straight back.'

'Thanks, Grey.'

'Kay?' Barnes emerged from the bedroom and held up a mobile phone.

'Is it password protected?'

'No.' He swiped the screen and accessed the recent calls log before passing it to Kay.

'Kevin McIntyre?'

'From his old work phone. Half an hour ago.'

'Christ, we're too late.'

263

Kay signed the crime scene register the uniformed officer thrust under her nose outside McIntyre's house, pulled on overalls and bootees and stomped her way into the hallway.

'Harriet? Where are you?'

'Living room.'

Kay pushed past one of the CSIs coming out of the room, and tried to calm her voice. It would do no good to panic; she had to remain focused, and she had to convey the urgency to Harriet and her team without disturbing the methodical way by which they were processing the room.

'I need to see the map and calculations that were on the coffee table,' she said. 'He's got another victim, and we need to find him now.'

Harriet's head snapped around to two CSIs who were huddled in one corner of the living room, carefully recording the evidence being seized. 'You two – where's the documentation DS Hunter needs?'

'Here,' said one of them.

'Thanks,' said Kay. She turned at the sound of a familiar voice in the hallway. 'Stay there, Dave.' She walked out of the house with Harriet in tow and reintroduced her to the BTP sergeant. 'I know there are already too many people at this crime scene, but Dave knows the network better than us.'

She handed over the maps and notebook to him, then stood at his side as he pulled on a pair of gloves and thumbed through the pages.

Each combination of notes comprised a sketch on the left-hand side of the notebook, with corresponding dates and times on the right-hand side. The sketches were made up of a series of straight lines, arrows between circles and, chillingly, a stick figure drawn next to one of the lines.

'Is this a kill diary?'

'I think this is McIntyre's way of working out the train times and speeds,' said Walker. 'These straight lines represent the tracks, the circles are stations, and the arrows have numbers next to them – the distance between stations.' He held up the folded map of the area that had pencilled arrows scrawled across its surface. 'It corresponds with this.'

'And the crosses are kill sites?'

'But retrospective, look.' He flicked back to the beginning. 'This is a rough drawing of what the site of Cameron Abbott's death looked like, but before that you've got pages of notes where he's researching the next location. Train times, visibility, ease of access to each site. Then on this page we've got the site where Nathan Cox was killed; a few pages later, Lawrence Whiting, and then Jason Evans most recently.'

'Does it show us where we'll find Peter Bailey?'

Walker pawed at the pages until he found the most recent entry. 'No – look, he's still working out where that location might be.'

'Can you work out from those where we might find him?'

'I'll have a go.'

She wanted to tell him to hurry, that another life was in danger, but she knew it wouldn't help. Instead, she paced the front garden, ignoring the damp air that swirled around her, and resisted the temptation to look at her watch.

All the murders had taken place during the commuter rush, in darkness, and they were running out of time.

'Got it.'

She hurried over to where Walker stood, his finger on a place on the map. 'The express from Victoria doesn't stop at this station.'

'Why there? Why now?'

'On an evening like this, if the station staff don't have to be out on the platform, they won't be – it's too cold. CCTV cameras are only placed at the car park and ticket office, and at the end of each platform.'

'Are you sure?'

His eyes met hers. 'Got any better ideas?'

'We can have uniformed cars attend other sites, if you think he'll be somewhere else.'

He rubbed his chin, and pointed to two more locations. 'Here. There are site works taking place at each of these – on the basis that's how he killed Jason Evans, we'll cover those as well. I can organise one of our patrols to go to this one, if you can manage a car to go to this other station, out at Harrietsham.'

Kay turned to Barnes. 'Radio it in. We need to move.'

————

Kay flung the car door shut and ran towards the entrance to the railway station, not waiting to see if Barnes was keeping up.

As she passed the ticket office and burst through onto the platform, she slid to a halt and listened.

'Anything?' Barnes murmured as he joined her.

'No. Split up?'

'Quicker. I'll take the other side.'

'There's a pedestrian crossing over there.'

'Got your radio to hand?'

'Yes.'

'Good. I don't trust this guy, Kay. Safety first, all right?'

'Okay.'

She watched Barnes jog away, his silhouette swallowed by the fog that was sweeping over the village, and then began to pace along the platform, sweeping her eyes over the dimly-lit buildings, and pulled out her mobile phone.

'Carys, it's me. Get on to the rail company. Tell them they need to stop all trains on the London to Maidstone line. Kevin McIntyre has got Peter Bailey, and we don't know where he is. We're trying to track him down.'

She ended the call and glanced up at the digital display above the platform that listed the next arrivals. An express train was scheduled to pass through the station within twenty minutes, destined for Ashford.

She had to find Bailey. She couldn't allow McIntyre to take another life.

'Anything?'

She jumped as her radio hissed with static, then brought it to her lips. 'Nothing. You?'

'No.'

'Can I help you?'

'Jesus.' Kay leapt away from the door that opened to her right, and glared at the bespectacled man who peered out at her.

'Sorry – I didn't mean to scare you. I saw you and your friend hanging around. What do you want?'

Kay held up her warrant card and caught her breath. 'We're looking for someone – have you seen anyone acting suspiciously around here since it got dark?'

'No, I've only seen the usual commuters that disembark. They don't hang about. They either have someone to collect them from the pick-up point outside, or they have their own cars.'

'Hang on.' Kay held up a finger to silence the station manager, and answered her mobile. 'Hunter.'

'Sarge? An off-duty officer has spotted McIntyre's car abandoned in the car park at West Malling station.'

Kay's throat tightened. 'Any sign of McIntyre?'

'No – how far away are you?'

'Five to ten minutes. Where's the officer now?'

'Waiting in the car park for you. He's on his motorbike and says if McIntyre gets in his car, he'll do his best to block it from leaving.'

'Radio Dave Walker to let him know, and arrange for a uniform car to get there as soon as possible. We're on our way.'

She ended the call, put her fingers between her lips and emitted a piercing whistle that reached the other platform and made the station master take two steps back.

'Barnes – we're leaving. Now!'

CHAPTER FORTY-NINE

Kay leapt from the car before Barnes had braked to a halt, and began to run.

Fog swirled around her ankles, the heavy damp air reducing the overhead lights to mere pinpricks and deadening any sounds.

McIntyre's car had been parked haphazardly into the nearest space to the railway station, with only one other car nearby.

The off-duty officer raised his hand in greeting as she approached.

'Stay with the car. Don't let him leave,' she yelled over her shoulder as she tore past, Barnes's footsteps in her wake.

Reaching the station buildings, she slid to a standstill as her eyes swept the empty platforms.

In the evening chill and poor light, the station held a ghostly quality to it, devoid of the commuters that would soon begin to arrive on the express services out of London. An eerie calm enclosed the unmanned buildings as they paced the platform, peering into dark corners and checking over their shoulders.

'Where are you, you bastard?'

'Christ, I can't see anything in this,' said Barnes. He pivoted and faced the opposite way, and then sighed and picked up his pace to catch up with her. 'Can you spot him?'

'No. How far away is Carys and the uniform car?'

'Only about ten minutes.'

'Dammit. We're going to lose him.' She quickly assessed the layout of the station. 'Right, you take this side of the platform, I'll take the other. If we don't find him here, we'll cross using the footbridge at the end and check the other side.'

'Got it.'

They split up, and Kay cast her eyes over the shadows between the aluminium benches bolted to the platform, checking door handles and working her way towards the far end.

Her mobile phone rang, and she silenced it quickly before putting it to her ear. 'Hello?'

'There's a train expected in less than five minutes,' said Walker. 'We're on our way, but it's not due to stop – it's an express service leaving Sevenoaks for Maidstone. There's no chance of him boarding it to escape.'

'Thanks.'

She ended the call and got her bearings.

The track to her left stretched out into the distance,

and she glanced into the darkened trench. No one moved. She shivered as the dankness of the night began to seep into her bones, chilling her to her core.

'Kay?'

'Yeah?'

Barnes moved between the ticket office and the toilet block, his silhouette out of proportion in the distorted light from the fluorescent beams that lit the platform amongst the encroaching fog. 'Anything?'

'No. Walker says there's an express train due any minute, but it won't stop here. Keep going.'

He nodded and moved away, and Kay resumed her search.

She reached the end of the toilet block and met him at the far end of the platform. 'Any luck?'

He shook his head.

'I can hear sirens.'

'Back up. At least we can widen the search area.'

Kay turned and squinted back along the platform, past the ticket office and towards the entrance to the car park. 'We didn't miss him, did we?'

'I don't think so. We'll try the other side.'

Kay spun round at a shout behind her, in time to see a figure tumble from the balustrade of the footbridge crossing the tracks above them.

A scream pierced the air.

'There!'

She broke away from Barnes, the sound of her footsteps thudding on the concrete surface creating a dull echo off the brickwork of the neighbouring ticket office. As she drew closer to the footbridge, she could see a man dangling from the railing that ran along the top of the balustrade, his legs swinging while he tried to find a foothold to haul himself back up.

In the distance, the familiar two-tone horn of an express train broke through the fog.

Kay grabbed the railing to swing herself around the corner as she bounded up the steps, only to see Kevin McIntyre's hands lose their grip, his screams deadened by the swirling fog.

'Barnes! With me!'

CHAPTER FIFTY

Kay launched herself at the balustrade, leaned over, and found herself staring into the eyes of Kevin McIntyre.

'Help me!'

He'd lost his grip on the railing, but now hung by his left hand from a cable that stretched the length of the footbridge. It dipped dangerously low, and Kay realised that if she didn't raise him up somehow, he'd be swept underneath the train when it shot underneath.

She reached out with both hands, wrapped her fingers around the thin material of the sleeves of his jacket, and tried to haul him back up.

She couldn't lift him.

Panicking, she glanced over her shoulder.

Barnes had reached the top of the steps, his hand on his side as he wheezed air back into his lungs.

'Ian – help!'

He jogged across to where she stood, peered over, and then grabbed McIntyre's right arm.

'Give me your other hand,' Kay yelled.

'I can't – you'll drop me.'

'No, we won't. You're hanging too low, Kevin. We need to raise you up. Give me your hand.'

Barnes checked over his shoulder. 'Jesus, the train's here, Kay!'

'I know – don't let go.'

The train horn sounded closer, behind them, and below their position the steel rails began to hum and throb with the motion of the approaching train.

McIntyre's fingers found hers, and then she leaned over and grabbed his wrist with her other hand, and between her and Barnes, they pulled him up so that his legs no longer hung beneath the bottom of the footbridge.

'Don't drop him, Barnes.'

'It would save some paperwork.'

'But it doesn't give his victims justice,' Kay snarled. 'I want this bastard alive.'

She gritted her teeth and braced herself against the edge of the pedestrian bridge. Her feet slid across the wet wooden panels, and then she felt the material of McIntyre's jacket give a little between her fingers.

The train driver blasted the horn, and over the noise she heard McIntyre scream.

The bridge structure shook with the force of the train's weight crossing the rails beneath, the lights above her swaying with the motion.

She heard Barnes growl between his teeth before he snatched at the man's wrists once more to try and get a better grip. Her own arms felt as if they were being wrenched from their sockets.

A wave of heat engulfed them as the locomotive went past underneath, the air making her eyes water before the roar of the engine passed.

A change in tone filled her ears as the first of the passenger carriages flew beneath them.

'Don't let me go! Please don't let me go!'

Kay tried to block out McIntyre's screams, and met Barnes's wide-eyed stare.

'He's slipping. I can't keep hold of him.'

'Hang on. Just a little longer – hang on.'

She twisted where she stood and tried to peer over the balustrade of the bridge and squinted beyond the reach of the spotlights, and into the darkness.

The train seemed to stretch forever, the carriages disappearing into the dark.

She wondered how it could be that whenever a train passed her on the track next to the motorway it could fly past in an instant, yet right now seem as if it was taking forever.

A tearing sound made her head whip back round, in time to see the material between her fingers rip apart.

'No!'

She grappled with the torn material until she could wrap her fingers around McIntyre's exposed bare wrists, and clung on.

He screamed again, his eyes full of terror as he tried to swing his legs away from the roof of the passing carriages.

Beyond where they stood, Kay became aware of shouting from the direction of the station buildings.

Carys propelled herself along the platform towards them, closely followed by Dave Walker and two other uniformed officers.

Barnes followed her gaze. 'They're not going to reach us in time.'

Kay cried out as McIntyre's wrists began to slide from her grip, his sweat greasing his skin.

She could smell the fear emanating from him, his eyes wide as he stared up at her, petrified.

'Don't let me go.'

'I won't.'

She averted her gaze and instead concentrated on willing all the strength she could muster. Beside her, Barnes grunted and shifted his weight. She sensed the strain being taken off her own arms, and then the roar of the train passed.

She lifted her head, to see the rear lights of the train disappearing through the station and into the fog.

'Come on, let's get you up,' said Barnes.

He was already pulling McIntyre back towards the railing, and Kay realised that without the force of the train passing beneath, McIntyre's body was no longer being dragged out of reach.

She gritted her teeth, leaned over, and grabbed the man's belt as Barnes heaved him over the edge.

He landed in a crumpled heap at their feet, and it was all Kay could do not to collapse next to him.

Instead, she propped herself up on shaking legs and

leaned against the side of the footbridge while Barnes crouched down and read McIntyre his rights.

'Kevin McIntyre, you're under arrest for the murders of Nathan Cox, Cameron Abbott—'

'It wasn't me – you've got this all wrong!'

'—Lawrence Whiting and Jason Evans. You do not have to say—'

'It's Alison's dad – he killed them all! Please – listen to me.' Kevin shrugged off Barnes's grip on his arm and glared at them both. 'I agreed to meet with him here. His car is in the car park near mine – I've been trying to work out who could be killing all our friends, and I made the mistake of trusting him. When we got here, he said to me he wanted to talk about Alison. He suggested we walk while we spoke.' He shook his head. 'I'm an idiot. I began to have doubts about my theory, and then when we got up here, he overpowered me.'

'Where's Peter Bailey?'

'I paid for him to stay at a motel in Ashford. He's safe. I told him not to go anywhere or answer his phone or the door. Not unless it was me.'

Kay narrowed her eyes. 'So, where's Martin Campbell?'

Kevin pointed over her shoulder into the darkness. 'He saw you coming, shoved me over the edge of the bridge, and then ran – he headed off down the tracks that way.'

CHAPTER FIFTY-ONE

'Stay here with him, Ian,' said Kay, and ran along the length of the footbridge.

She tore down the steps as fast as she could, nearly colliding with Carys at the bottom.

'It's Alison's dad, Martin Campbell. He's our killer. Come with me. You two – tell that off-duty officer to stay here and make sure Campbell doesn't try to escape back along the platforms or get back to his car. Have you got torches we can use?'

'Here.'

'Thanks. Radio through and get a car over to Campbell's house. Have them get a search warrant organised and secure the scene. They'll need to question his wife as well. Get yourselves up to the main road in case he tries to climb up the embankment from the railway.'

'Will do.'

The two uniformed officers handed over the torches before running back to their car, the older of the two with his radio to his mouth.

Kay spun on her heel and crouched down, dropping to the tracks before helping Carys, and then the pair began to run in the direction McIntyre had indicated.

'What if he's lying, Kay?'

'Can't take that risk. I thought I saw someone up on the bridge with McIntyre but I couldn't be sure because of the fog. If that person is innocent, why run?'

In response, Carys cursed as she stumbled on one of the sleepers.

'Careful! The third rail is electrified. Slow down.'

They continued to sweep their torch beams across the undergrowth to either side of the track, their breathing the only sound in the still of the night.

'I can imagine what Larch said when he found out we wanted the train stopped.'

'They haven't stopped them.'

Kay swung around. 'What you mean, they haven't stopped the trains? I thought that was the last one to go through here?'

'I'm sorry, Sarge. Sharp tried his best, so did Dave Walker. Larch said you don't have a strong enough case to stop the trains. They cost too much money. If you're wrong, Larch said there could be all sorts of political fallout. He says we have no proof apart from an abandoned car that our suspect is here.'

'Hold my torch.' Kay turned her mobile phone in her hand and hit the speed dial.

Sharp answered within seconds. 'Where are you?'

'Martin Campbell is the killer. He threw McIntyre over a footbridge. McIntyre's with Barnes now. Carys and I are trying to catch up with Martin Campbell. What's this about the trains not being stopped?'

'Larch says he'll only arrange for the trains to be stopped if he can be convinced the killer is there. I'm sorry, Kay. Where are you now?

'On the bloody tracks.'

'Why?'

'Because Martin Campbell took off along here only a few minutes ago. I'm in pursuit with Carys. You have to stop the trains.'

There was a rustling sound at the end of the line, and Kay realised she had been on speakerphone all the time. The next voice she heard was Larch's.

'You have no proof that Martin Campbell is your killer. Return to Barnes and arrest McIntyre.'

'McIntyre was hanging from the footbridge when we found him. He nearly died,' Kay yelled. 'What more proof do you bloody need?'

She ended the call, fuming.

'I can't see anything in this fog,' Carys muttered.

'Me neither.' Kay cursed. 'If we don't find him, we'll have to put out a request for everyone to be on the lookout for him at ports and airports. Ashford International station, too. It wouldn't surprise me if he tried to make a run for it over the Channel.'

'At least he can't get too far too fast – his car's still back at the station.'

Kay's torch beam bobbed over the rails as she swept it across her line of vision, and she glanced over her shoulder.

The mottled lights from the railway station illuminated the ghostly form of the footbridge in the distance, and the damp air clung to her skin and hair.

Doubt began to claw at her mind.

Had she really seen a second figure on the footbridge, or had the fog obliterated her view so much that she'd been mistaken.

What if McIntyre was lying?

What if he wasn't?

The unmistakeable sound of a train horn cut through the fog.

'Off the tracks, Carys.'

They moved to the wayside, the uneven ballast slowing their progress.

Kay led the way, keeping her torch lowered so they could watch where they trod, while Carys swept hers from side to side, illuminating the sides of the embankment. Kay lifted her eyes and swallowed.

A smaller bridge rose out of the gloom ahead, the cutting underneath it narrow and steep.

She checked over her shoulder.

No trains approached the station from behind.

Decision time.

If they entered the cutting and were still there when the train roared through, they'd only have the other track to move on to.

If another train was coming from the opposite direction, they'd have nowhere to go.

If they didn't enter the cutting, they might never catch up with Campbell.

Carys bumped into her.

'Kay?'

She shook her head. 'We're going to have to wait here until the train passes.'

The ballast began to shake and shift under her feet, and she threw out her arms to steady herself as the rails started to sing.

Carys cried out, and then the beam from her torch spun in the air and then went out.

'Shit, sorry – I've lost my torch!'

Her voice was muffled in the thick air, but Kay could hear the sense of panic.

'It's okay. We've still got this one.'

A branch cracked a few metres along the track in front of them, and Kay swung the beam around.

A figure stepped into the torchlight, his right foot hovering over the third rail.

'Martin, move away from the rail.'

He emitted a shaking breath, his shoulders slumped.

Kay held up a hand to shield her eyes from the headlights of the oncoming train, and began to walk towards him. She realised the driver wouldn't see him until the last minute; visibility was so bad.

The train would be moving at a slower pace due to the weather, but it was still too fast. The railway company had a timetable to keep, if it was going to convey its passengers home on time.

'Martin, move out of the way,' she yelled. We need to talk.'

'There's nothing to say.'

Kay picked up her pace, the sound of her and Carys's shoes crunching across the ballast now diminishing in the wake of the enormous force bearing down on them at speed.

'There's nothing to talk about,' he shouted.

She stopped within a metre of him, and checked to her right.

The train's headlights now clearly illuminated the track where Campbell stood, and the sound of the horn blasted through the night air.

A screech of brakes reached her ears, but she knew it would be no good.

The train wouldn't stop in time.

She had seconds.

She reached out her hand and shouted over the noise of the train as the driver hit the horn once more. 'Martin, please!'

His face blank, he turned back to face the oncoming train.

Kay cursed under her breath. If she tried to grab him and he overpowered her, they'd both be sucked under the train, and she had no wish to die today.

But she did want justice.

'He's going to get away with it!'

Carys brushed past her.

Before Kay could react, the young detective launched herself at Martin and barrelled into him, knocking him over as the front of the locomotive roared past and they disappeared from view.

Kay screamed.

'Carys – no!'

CHAPTER FIFTY-TWO

Kay paced the wayside, the flash of light from the first passenger carriage creating a strobe effect around her while the people inside looked up askance at the train's sudden braking motion.

She locked eyes with one of them as he looked out the window, his mouth distorting into an "o" of shock when he registered the pale face that flashed past his field of vision.

'Come on,' she muttered.

She couldn't risk moving any closer to the tracks to check underneath – not that she wanted to contemplate what she would see.

Kay pushed her hair out of her face, the downdraught from the train tugging at her clothing and filling her nostrils with hot air that held a remnant of oil and grease. She swallowed, trying to counteract the fear and the bile that threatened to rise.

She had to hope.

She turned away in an effort to shield her ears as the driver increased the pressure on the brakes, the loud squealing boring into her skull while she tried to retain her balance on the uneven ballast that bucked under the weight of the train. She pointed her torch towards the ground, making sure she was nowhere near the live rail and then swung it round so she could count the carriages that passed.

The light rebounded off the thick fog around her, the liveried sides of the carriages a blur that emerged from the cutting before the back of the train roared past, its rear lights an explosive red beacon in the fog as it finally began to decelerate.

Kay's attention snapped back to the bare tracks in front of her.

There was no sign of Carys, or Martin Campbell.

She ran a hand over her mouth, stepped onto the track, and checked there wasn't a train approaching from the opposite direction, before sweeping her torch over the rails.

No clothing. No sign of anything. Or anyone.

She raised her gaze to the back of the train, and fought back a whimper.

Was it possible for two people to be swept away by the force of the train? The horrifying thought that the young detective could be trapped underneath one of the carriages turned her stomach.

How would she ever face the woman's parents to tell them their daughter had been so intent on proving herself to her colleagues that she'd risked everything to bring a suspect to justice?

She ran along the sleepers towards the rear of the train, its mechanical parts clicking and creaking as it cooled after such a rapid deceleration.

A chill began to crawl down her neck.

Reaching the back of the train, she turned and began to wave the beam from left to right over the tracks between the train and her original position.

She pushed the memory of Lawrence Whiting's remains to the back of her mind, and concentrated instead on the detritus to each side of the track that had been thrown from the road above the cutting by passing motorists and fly-tippers. Each time the beam fell upon an item of clothing, she moved closer to check it didn't resemble the trouser suit Carys had been wearing, and moved on.

Approaching the point where she and the detective constable had been standing when the train had passed by, she stopped.

'Where are you, C—'

A groan emanated from the undergrowth in front of her, and she stepped back in shock.

She aimed the torch beam left and right, trying to locate the origin of the sound, but it was impossible in the poor light.

Then, movement, and a trouser-clad leg raised into the air as someone tried to right themselves.

Another groan.

Kay held the torch higher and made her way forward, her brow creasing.

Was it possible—?

'Get off of me, you bitch.'

Carys's head emerged from the undergrowth, and then the rest of her as she rolled into a crouching position. 'Stay where you are, Mr Campbell. You're under arrest.'

Kay's jaw dropped open as she neared.

Carys had landed on top of Martin Campbell and now had him face-down in the bracken, reading him his rights.

Relief shot through her system, and she crouched down to help Carys to her feet, and then Campbell.

Keeping a firm grip on Campbell's arm, she quickly assessed the scratches to the detective constable's face. 'Anything broken?'

'I don't think so,' Carys said, her voice breathless. She reached up to straighten her hair, and Kay noticed the woman's hands shaking.

She had to get her checked out by a doctor as soon as possible, to make sure she wasn't going to go into shock.

She glanced up at the sound of sirens, and familiar blue flashing lights appeared on the bridge above them moments before the sound of screeching tyres reached her.

'Cavalry's here,' she said, and turned her attention back to Campbell. 'Come on.'

She took him by the arm and frogmarched him over the tracks, careful to ensure he didn't purposely step on the live third rail, and shoved him towards the embankment.

'Climb.'

She scrambled up the steep slope beside him, and kept a guiding hand on his arm as they progressed towards the road above. At one point, as she reached out to steady him, he snatched his arm away.

'Don't touch me.'

Kay bit back the urge to push him to the bottom of the cutting, and instead breathed a sigh of relief as they reached the barbed wire fencing that separated the railway land from the patrol car.

Two uniformed officers climbed out of the vehicle as a second patrol drew to a standstill behind theirs, and began to make their way across the road to meet Kay. One of them pulled out a pair of wire cutters and began to snip away at the fencing until they had a hole big enough to climb through.

Kay pushed Campbell towards the two uniformed officers and then turned back to help Carys.

'My legs won't stop shaking,' she mumbled.

Reaching the top, Kay waited while Campbell was handcuffed and led to the first vehicle, and then reached out and helped Carys towards the second.

'Carys?'

'Yes, Sarge?'

'Don't ever scare me like that again.'

CHAPTER FIFTY-THREE

Kay grabbed a bottle of water and her notes from her
desk in the incident room before hurrying towards the
interview suites on the ground floor.

Swiping her card across the security panel, she heard
someone ending a phone call before Larch emerged
from one of the meeting rooms, a harried expression on
his face.

She checked to make sure the corridor was empty
behind her, and then stalked up to him and stabbed her
finger at his chest.

'You've gone too far. Sir.'

He looked down at her hand and then back to her.
He cocked an eyebrow. 'I've got no idea what you're
talking about, Detective Sergeant Hunter. Are you
threatening me?'

'You put our lives at risk out there. You didn't stop
the trains. We nearly lost an officer today because of
your actions. I don't care if you've got a personal

vendetta against me, sir, but I do care when you put one of my officers, one of my colleagues, at risk.'

His eyes narrowed. 'It was your decision to pursue the suspect. You were the most senior officer at the scene. It was your responsibility to ensure she was safe. As it is, I understand that Detective Constable Miles had a very lucky escape.' He swiped her hand out of the way. 'Be careful, Hunter. You're walking on thin ice.'

She stormed past, knowing in her heart she'd made a mistake to let her emotions get the better of her, but unable to excuse her DCI's choice to gamble with their lives to prove a point.

She took a moment to compose herself, adjusted her suit jacket, and looked up as Barnes appeared.

She took a deep breath. 'Let's do this.'

When she entered the interview room, Martin Campbell was engrossed in a conversation with his solicitor.

His own clothes had been removed when he had been booked in by the custody sergeant, and he now wore standard issue coveralls and soft slip-on shoes. Cuts and scratches covered his face where he had tumbled into the undergrowth with Carys, and despite the fact he ran his hand over his hair every few minutes, it remained unruly.

The two men fell silent as the door opened, and Kay raised her eyebrows. The solicitor nodded to her and turned his attention back to the papers spread before him. Kay and Barnes settled into their seats and she began the recording. After asking Campbell to confirm his name and address, she began the formal interview.

'Mr Campbell, please can you explain why you chose to run earlier tonight?'

'I thought it was that madman McIntyre chasing me. I had to get away.'

'That would be the same Kevin McIntyre that you pushed over a footbridge at West Malling station?'

'He fell. There was a struggle. He tried to throw me over the parapet. I managed to get away from him, and I ran. He's a madman. I thought he was going to kill me.'

He crossed his hands on the table in front of him, and Kay pointed to his right hand.

'You appear to have ripped the nail on your middle finger.'

'I do a lot of woodwork at home.' He shrugged. 'It happens.'

Kay leaned forward in her seat. 'I don't believe you, Mr Campbell. You see, our crime scene investigators found the remnants of a fingernail in the bindings that were used to tie Lawrence Whiting to the train tracks. The swabs our custody team took from you upon your arrival here last night have been passed on for comparative analysis. I'm willing to bet the DNA will match yours.'

Campbell's mouth worked, but no sound came out. He recovered quickly, and snorted. 'This is preposterous. Kevin McIntyre is the man you should be questioning. I had nothing to do with the murder of Lawrence Whiting. I didn't even know the man.'

'But you made sure that you got to know him, didn't you? That's how you managed to entice him to meet with you. How did it work? Did you phone him to tell him that you wanted to talk about Alison, for old times' sake?'

His bluster wavered. 'I don't know what you're talking about.'

'Mr Campbell, our officers are attending your house at the moment. We have a warrant to search the premises. Is there anything you would like to tell us?'

His eyes narrowed and he jerked forward in his seat.

His solicitor put a restraining hand on his arm.

Barnes turned a page of his notebook. 'All the murders carried out on that stretch of railway involved a lot of planning and a lot of time. That sort of planning takes dedication. Someone who kills like that is dealing with a lot of rage. Were you angry that Alison died?'

'Of course I was bloody angry.'

'Were you angry enough to seek revenge? Did you blame them all for her death?'

Campbell said nothing, and swallowed.

Kay reached into the folder under her elbow and pulled out a report. 'This is a copy of the coroner's inquest. How did it make you feel when the coroner ruled her death as accidental, and you had no one to blame?'

'The coroner was wrong. It's the railway company's fault she died. They're the ones that got away with murder.'

'The thing is, Mr Campbell, it wasn't accidental death.'

'What do you mean?'

'We have a witness statement from Peter Bailey, one of Alison's colleagues. Unfortunately, for reasons unknown to us at this time, Mr Bailey wasn't requested to give evidence at the inquest. Mr Bailey maintains that it wasn't an accident that Alison died.'

'Of course it wasn't,' said Campbell. He leaned back in his seat and threw his hands up. 'That's what I've been trying to tell everybody since the inquest. It wasn't an accident, because their negligence resulted in Alison's death.'

Kay shook her head. 'No one is to blame for Alison's death. Peter Bailey explained to us that Alison chose to walk in front of that train. She killed herself.'

A choked cry escaped Campbell's lips, and his solicitor frowned.

'I'd like ten minutes with my client alone.'

Kay leaned forward and terminated the interview recording.

CHAPTER FIFTY-FOUR

Kay entered the second interview suite and found Carys waiting along with Kevin McIntyre and the solicitor he'd nominated.

'You've got some explaining to do,' she said as she lowered herself into the seat next to Carys and nodded at the detective constable to begin recording.

Kay read McIntyre the legal caution, and launched into her questions.

'What on earth were you thinking?'

The man wiped at his eyes. 'I wanted to stop him. I knew I didn't have enough evidence to say anything to the police, especially after Cameron reported me for harassment.'

'What happened there? Why did he report you for harassment?'

'I tried to warn him. I had a feeling Martin was somehow involved in Nate's death, but Cameron wouldn't believe me. He said I was hysterical because the railway company was exonerated from any blame in Alison's death. I tried to tell him that wasn't the point, but he wouldn't listen. I tried phoning him to start off with, but then he blocked my number. I knew where he lived, and so I went around there a couple of times but he yelled at me – I didn't want to make a scene in front of the neighbours. I tried once more, but that's when he reported me to the police. I was going to write to him, to tell him what I'd found out, but it was too late – he was killed before I got the chance.'

'What made you suspect Martin was involved in the deaths of Nathan and Cameron?'

He leaned back in his chair. 'It was something he said after the inquest. When we were leaving the building, there were some reporters outside, but he got Karen past those, and as he got into the car that was waiting for them, he turned to me and said he'd have to take matters into his own hands. At first, I thought he was going to ask for a second inquest – but that never happened. Two months later, Nathan was dead.' He looked down at his hands. 'I know everyone said it was suicide, but I knew Nate – Alison and I had socialised with him, and he didn't seem the sort to do that. I saw him during the inquest, and he seemed pretty composed. Shocked and upset, yes – but not suicidal.'

'Why did Alison kill herself, Kevin? What did you argue about that morning?'

Tears spilled over his cheeks. 'I was an idiot. When I finished my last engineering contract, the company I worked for didn't have anything else for me to do, so they seconded me to the business development team. There was a team building weekend away in Surrey. I got too drunk, and so did one of the regional sales reps. She was pretty, and I was too dumb to say "no".' He blinked, then used the sleeve of his shirt to wipe his eyes. 'It only happened once, but when she found out I was getting married, she became spiteful and threatened to tell Alison. I couldn't let Ali hear it from a complete stranger, so I told her.'

'When?'

'The morning she walked out in front of the train. She stormed out of the house. I tried to get her to come back, to tell her that it'd never happened again – that it shouldn't have happened at all, but she wouldn't listen—'

Kay let him have a moment to compose himself before proceeding. 'Kevin, we've seen all your notes and maps at your house. What's all that about?'

'I was trying to catch him. It's all my fault he's doing this. The inquest said it was accidental death, so the railway company's not to blame. Martin always maintained Alison's colleagues should have done something to save her, but how could they? He blamed them – said they should've done more to stop her.'

'Did he know about your affair?'

'No. Not until last night.' He leaned across, plucked two tissues from the box on the table, and blew his nose. 'When I first confronted him in the car park at the station, he told me he was going to hand himself in. Said he wanted to explain why he'd done it first, and so I agreed to walk with him while he talked.' He scrunched up the tissues and balled them into his fist. 'Stupid of me. I should've realised he'd found out I was trying to warn Peter. He was livid when I told him I knew what he was doing, and that I'd go to the police if he didn't. I had Peter's evidence by then that Martin had contacted him and wanted to meet him alone.'

'What happened?'

'You saw what happened. He went berserk. By then, we were up on the footbridge – originally, Martin had suggested we walk along it because we were still talking. We were about halfway across when I told him about my affair. That's when he barged into me and I lost my footing. I don't know how, but he managed to tip me over the side, and then he ran.'

Kay leaned back in her seat. She'd seen it time and again as a uniformed officer patrolling the centre of Maidstone when the pubs and clubs had emptied out into the streets in the early hours of the morning – the slightest person fuelled by anger often didn't know their own strength.

McIntyre put his head in his hands, a sob escaping his lips. 'It's all my fault. She lost the will to live because of me, and now they're all dead.'

Kay rose from her seat and stopped the recording after noting the interview had concluded.

It was time to charge their suspect.

CHAPTER FIFTY-FIVE

Kay held the door open for Barnes, and then made her way over to the seats opposite where Martin Campbell and his solicitor sat.

Campbell's demeanour had changed. Where once he had been defiant, an air of righteousness about him, there was now doubt. Sweat glistened on his forehead as he repeatedly ran his hand through his hair, and even his solicitor appeared wary, unsure as to the true state of his client's mind.

Kay leaned over and pressed the record button, glanced up to make sure the CCTV camera in the interview room showed a red light under its lens, and began.

After formally cautioning Campbell once more, she leaned back and observed the man in front of her.

Since she'd first met him, he'd visibly deteriorated.

Where once he'd seemed to her to be dignified in his

grief, concerned for his wife and devastated at his daughter's death, she now saw him for what he was.

A conniving, evil murderer who took pleasure in watching his victims die a painful and terrifying death.

'How did you find out about Peter Bailey? His name wasn't mentioned in the coroner's report.'

'I didn't know about him until Lawrence said I should speak to him. I had no idea he was there at the time of Alison's death. I knew about all the others of course, from the inquest.' His eyes fell to his hands in his lap. 'Karen and I went every day to the hearing. I hated them all. They all sat there, crying as the coroner asked them about the accident. None of them told me she killed herself.'

'I don't think they wanted to believe it themselves. Peter Bailey was the one standing nearest to her when it happened.'

Campbell raised his eyes and placed his hands on the table in front of him, his fists clenched. 'They should've still done something to stop her.'

'Martin, we've found the model railway. There are notebooks with your writing in—'

He gasped, his face turning white.

Kay folded her hands on the table. 'You tried to rub out any trace of your notes, but the indentations are still visible. Why did you do it, Martin?'

He wiped his eyes. 'After the inquest, Karen and I retreated into our own little world. You've seen how Karen is – she doesn't even know what day of the week it is most of the time, she's so full of antidepressants. I was scared I was going to lose her, too. You've got no idea – you didn't see her when Alison was still alive. She was so vibrant, so joyful to be around. I had to do something. I had to teach them a lesson. Alison was the junior member of the team, and they'd let her die. She was my little girl. They made her out to be clumsy and unprofessional at the inquest. It wasn't true. Those men, the ones that were there that day, they should have been looking out for her.'

'How did you manage to convince them to meet with you?'

'It was easy. I still had Alison's phone with all their contact details in. I used her phone to call them, knowing they'd pick up to find out who was on the other end. I asked if they wanted to meet for a quiet drink somewhere. Somewhere where I wasn't known. Away from the railway tracks – I knew you lot would probably interview anyone within a hair's breadth of where I killed them. Karen's antidepressants are strong. All I had to do was slip some into their drink. I always waited until their second one, so they'd be less on their guard. They'd start to feel drowsy within moments and so I'd suggest I drive them home. Of course, they accepted.'

'Except you didn't drive them home, did you? You took them to where you'd already decided you'd kill them.'

'They deserved it.'

'How did you gain access to the site where you killed Jason Evans? The area was cordoned off with security fencing.'

He smirked. 'After Alison died, her employers wanted nothing to do with us. They were too busy preparing for the inquest and working out how to ensure they didn't take the blame. They shunned us – I think we were an embarrassment to them.' He glanced down at his fingernails. 'When the funeral director got in touch with us and asked us to collect Alison's effects, there was a key amongst her belongings. Turns out it's a master key for all the railway company's sites up and down the network – it saves them having to have separate keys for different places.'

'So you kept it. How on earth did you think you'd get away with murdering these poor men?' Kay spread the photographs of the project team out in front of him.

A faint smile crossed his lips, and then he frowned. 'It was easy, at first. They were all suffering from depression after Alison's death, so it was simple enough to make it look like they'd killed themselves.'

'Except it went wrong with Lawrence Whiting, didn't it?'

Campbell clenched his fists. 'I got the dose wrong. I didn't realise he'd put on so much weight since I'd last seen him at the inquest. It seems he consoled himself with food, as well as antidepressants.' He glared at Kay. 'It would still have worked perfectly, though. He wasn't going to escape.'

'Except a witness heard him shouting.'

'Like I said, they all deserved what they got.'

'No,' said Kay, 'they didn't. None of them did, did they? Because Alison killed herself.'

'I didn't know.'

'That's no excuse. We spoke to Peter. He says he's always maintained that Alison stepped into the path of that train by choice. Kevin McIntyre had an affair, Alison found out, and killed herself. And despite the fact by your own admission you'd killed four men, you decided you wouldn't stop there, and you'd try to kill Kevin McIntyre as well.'

'Yes. He cheated on my little girl. The bastard deserved it.'

The duty solicitor rolled his eyes and slapped his notebook down on the desk. Kay ignored him and kept her eyes trained on Campbell.

'Kevin had already discovered that you were responsible for killing the rest of Alison's project team.'

Campbell sat back in his seat, his look of defiance slipping. 'Yes.'

'So, how did you persuade him to meet you?'

'I told him I was going to hand myself in. That I couldn't live with the guilt. That I wanted a chance to explain to him why I'd done what I'd done.'

'What changed?'

His eyes narrowed. 'Nothing. He had to die.'

CHAPTER FIFTY-SIX

Kay inserted her key into the shiny new lock and pushed the front door open, kicked her shoes off and dropped her bag on the bottom tread of the stairs, and then padded through to the kitchen.

Adam looked up from the weekly free newspaper he'd spread out on the kitchen worktop, and smiled.

'Got him?'

'Got him.'

He slid from the wooden stool and cleared the space between them in four long strides, pulling her into a hug. 'Well done.'

She sank into his embrace for a moment, before gently pulling away, tears in her eyes.

'Hey, what's wrong?'

She wiped at her cheeks. 'Gavin's in hospital, and it's all my fault.'

Adam frowned, then took her by the hand and led

her over to the central aisle and pulled out another stool for her. 'Sit. What's going on?'

She leaned her elbows on the worktop and ran her hand through her hair before telling Adam about using Gavin's computer to continue her investigation after their house had been burgled, only to find out the next day that her swipe card hadn't worked, and then discovering that Gavin had been attacked that night on his way home.

'How is he?'

She sniffed. 'Two broken ribs, a broken nose, and concussion. The hospital sent him home earlier today.'

'It could be a coincidence.'

She let out a shaking breath. 'What if it's not?'

'Does he have any idea who attacked him?'

'No, and I spoke to the detective investigating it – there's nothing captured on CCTV. It's as if whoever attacked him knew exactly where the cameras were.'

Adam ran a hand across a stubbled chin. 'Maybe you should drop it.'

'I can't,' said Kay. 'All of this, it proves that I'm right, doesn't it? Someone doesn't want me to find out the truth.'

'But are you any closer to finding out who?'

She shook her head and lowered her gaze. 'When I logged in, the records had been deleted. There's no sign of that gun ever being seized or taken into evidence.'

'Jesus, Kay.'

'This is bigger than trying to set me up. There's

something else going on, and I can't find a way in. I can't find *anything*.'

Adam reached out and took her hands between his. 'I've always believed in you, you know I have. And I know it was my idea to find out who was behind your Professional Standards investigation, but our house has been burgled—'

'They didn't take anything—'

'—to scare us, if nothing else, and Gavin's been beaten up. This goes way beyond evidence tampering, Kay. Someone is trying to stop you. Maybe you should listen.'

She sighed and slipped her hands from his, and rubbed at her eye. 'Is that what you really think?'

'I'm scared what they'll do to you if you don't stop.'

'I know.'

A loud whine from behind them interrupted her thoughts, and a smile broke across Adam's face.

'In other news, Holly is a mum.'

'What? When?'

Kay leapt from the kitchen stool and dashed round to where Adam sat.

He pointed to Holly's bed, where four tiny wriggling forms curled up next to the huge dog, who stared up at them with deep dark eyes, her tongue lolling out.

Kay crossed her arms over her chest. 'Well, you do look pleased with yourself, Holly.' She glanced over her shoulder. 'How old are they?'

'Born at ten o'clock this morning. No complications,

so I've phoned the family – they'll be here in a bit to collect her and take them all home.'

Kay bent down and patted the huge dog on the head. 'Good girl,' she said, and stroked Holly's head. Her eyes fell to the puppies suckling and tumbling over each other. 'They're so tiny.'

'They'll grow up fast enough. Maurice, the owner, has had Great Danes before, so he knows what he's doing.'

'I might go and get changed before he gets here.'

'No problem.'

She kissed him on the way past, and then picked up her bag and shoes and climbed the stairs before making her way along the landing to their bedroom. She undressed, then moved into the en suite and turned on the taps.

A loud sob escaped her lips, and she allowed herself a couple of minutes to let it all out before splashing her face with cold water and drying her eyes.

She glared at herself in the mirror over the small sink.

'Get a grip,' she said. 'You can't be jealous of a dog.'

She heard the doorbell ring and hurried into the bedroom, throwing on jeans and a sweatshirt before running downstairs and into the kitchen, where Adam was talking to Holly's owner and his son.

'We've told Alec he's allowed to keep one,' said Maurice. He ruffled his son's hair. 'Have you made up your mind?'

'This one. She's really nice. And she doesn't give up – look.' The boy pointed out the tiny puppy that was now fighting its way over its siblings to get closer to its mother.

'Thought of a name?' said Kay.

Alec grinned. 'Hunter,' he said.

Adam snorted. 'Well you're going to have your hands full, that's for sure.'

'Oi.' Kay slapped his arm, then turned back to Alec. 'That's very nice of you, thank you.'

'We should get going.' Maurice held his hand out to Adam, and then Kay. 'Thanks for everything. I knew she'd be in safe hands.'

'No problem,' said Adam. 'She was an absolute dream to deal with. You've got my number. Don't hesitate to call if you need to.'

'Ah, we'll try to let you get your life back,' Maurice grinned. 'When do you want to see her at the surgery?'

'I'll be back in on Monday, so if you phone Anna and get an appointment then, that'll be fine.'

Kay helped Alec gather the four puppies and placed them in the carry box, and Adam handed Holly's lead to Maurice before giving the dog's ears a rub.

'Well done, Holly,' he said.

They stood on the doorstep as the family waved goodbye, then watched the tail lights of the car recede down the street.

'Come on,' said Adam. 'It's wine o'clock.'

He kissed her cheek then moved away, his footsteps padding back to the kitchen.

'Yeah.' Kay swept her eyes over the street, seeking out the shadows between the streetlights.

Who was watching? Were they out there, waiting for another opportunity?

She wouldn't be stopped, not now. She owed Gavin that much.

She had to find out who had attacked him.

She turned her back and slammed the door, sliding the new bolts across the top and bottom of the frame.

She straightened, then reached into her jeans pocket, her fist clenching around the USB stick.

'I'll get you, you bastards.'

FROM THE AUTHOR

Dear Reader,

Thank you for choosing to read *Will to Live*. I hope you enjoyed the second in the Detective Kay Hunter series.

If you did enjoy it, I'd be grateful if you could write a review. It doesn't have to be long, just a few words, but it really is the best way for me to help new readers discover one of my books for the first time.

If you'd like to stay up to date with my new releases, as well as exclusive competitions and giveaways, you're welcome to join my Reader Group at my website, www.rachelamphlett.com.

I will never share your email address, and you can unsubscribe at any time.

You can also contact me via Facebook, Twitter, or by email.

I love hearing from readers – I read every message and will always reply.

Thanks again for your support.

Best wishes,
Rachel Amphlett

CPSIA information can be obtained
at www.ICGtesting.com
Printed in the USA
LVHW030158250723
753385LV00024B/1288